BRIDGERS 5: THE TRIAL OF EXTINCTION

STAN C. SMITH

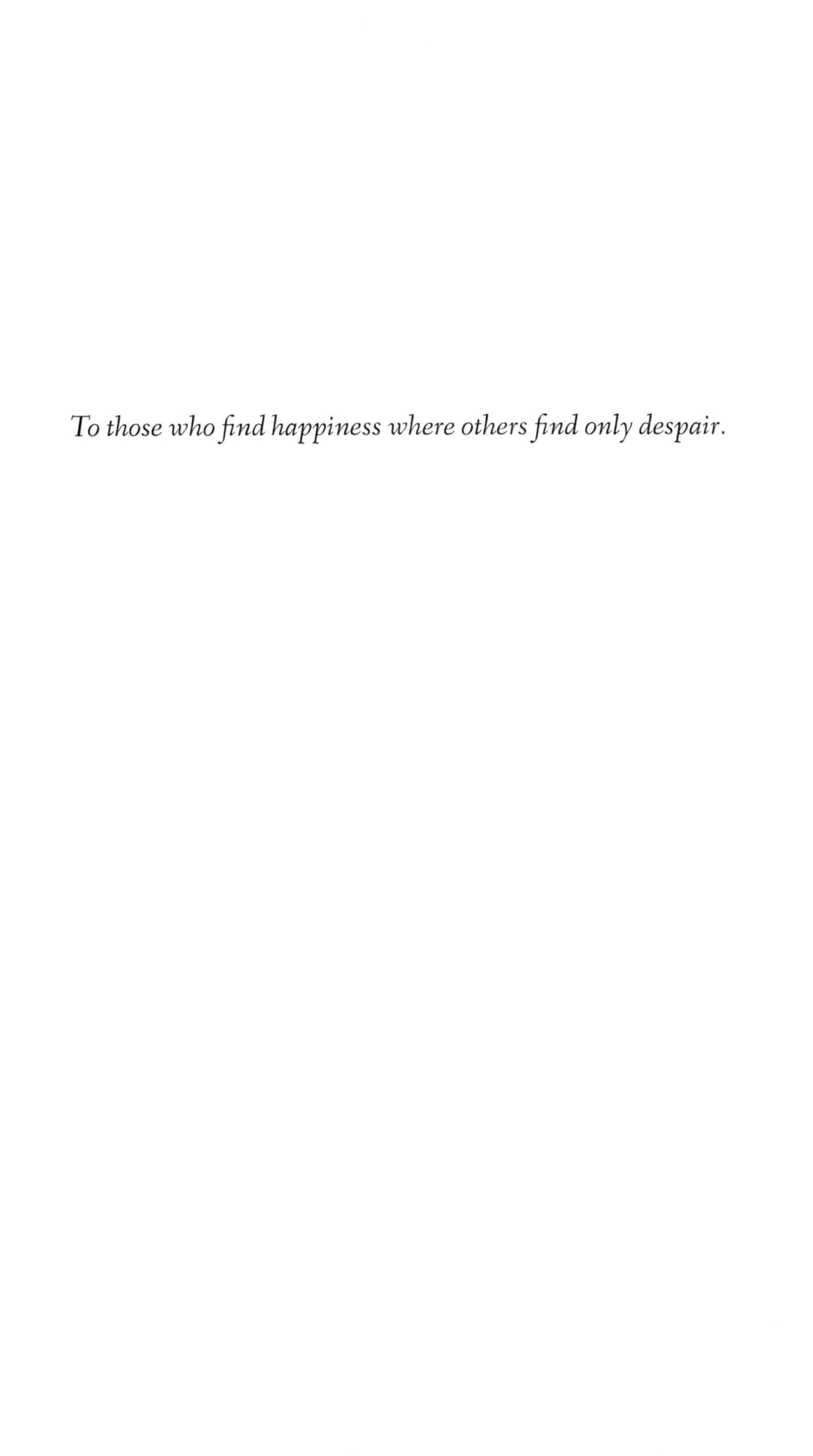

To those who find happiness where others find only despair.

THE TRIAL OF EXTINCTION

We're all put on trial at some point. Maybe we'll be found guilty, or maybe we'll be found innocent. Either way, what we've done cannot be undone.

INFINITY FOWLER

1

———

RUMBLES

APRIL 10 - Before sunrise

INFINITY FOWLER GLANCED up at the stars just as the first hint of sunlight began spreading across the eastern sky. She sensed that something wasn't right. The air felt dry, almost prickly, as if the static electricity might make her hair stand on end at any moment. The sounds were different, too. No, not different—missing entirely. Normally, in the minutes before sunrise, she could hear the deep thrumming of billions of winged arthropods gearing up for a new day, vibrating their wings to warm their bodies. She would also hear endless layers of chirps, trills, and buzzes as creatures both large and small attempted to attract mates. But this morning the landscape was silent.

Infinity closed her eyes and tried to resume her meditation. She slowed her breathing, focusing on the path of each breath as it made its way into her lungs, where the air's oxygen was exchanged for her body's carbon dioxide waste. She held each breath for nearly a full minute, which was easy because the atmosphere on this version of Earth contained more oxygen than the air on her own world.

Her skin prickled. She cursed silently and opened her eyes. A flash of light from above caught her attention. She glanced up and her chest clenched tight. "What the hell?" she said aloud, although she was alone on the rocky hillside.

A green glow was fluttering almost directly above her, high in the atmosphere. The glow began to expand, stretching to the east and to the west in a throbbing line, like a row of dancing green spirits. The glow quickly reached the horizon in both directions, then it began expanding north and south, adding spectacular columns of red and orange alongside the original row of green.

Infinity got to her feet. "No, no, no. This can't be happening." The dancing lights were now covering the entire sky. It was a massive aurora borealis—northern lights. She only knew this because she had witnessed such displays on her own version of Earth in the months leading up to the planet's destruction. Auroras had become more frequent and more expansive toward the end, but even in the last few days of Earth's existence, she hadn't seen anything as spectacular as this.

Another movement caught her eye, this time a dark splotch to the east, standing out against the glowing sky. The splotch was getting larger, changing shape, its edges surging and shrinking. Infinity could hear waves of clicking and fluttering, which grew louder as the dark cloud expanded. She realized the cloud wasn't growing—it was getting closer. It was a swarm of winged creatures. The clicking and fluttering continued to grow until its roar was deafening.

The creatures didn't rise as they closed in on the hillside. Instead, they flew directly into the sheets of bedrock and patches of moss. Thousands of pigeon-sized bugs began smashing into the hillside around Infinity. She dropped to her knees and covered her head with her arms. One of the creatures hit her neck, knocking her onto her stomach. She pulled her legs underneath herself, trying to make her body a smaller target. Still she took another half dozen hits as the suicidal creatures rammed full speed into her back.

Finally, the bombardment stopped. Infinity opened her eyes and sat up. The hillside around her was covered with the broken bodies of a type of creature she had never seen during the nineteen months she and the other colonists had lived on this world. Whatever the creatures were, something had screwed with their ability to navigate.

The rising of another sound drew Infinity's attention to the slope behind and above her—the pounding of heavy, chitinous feet against bedrock. Six black tiger beetles, each weighing at least four hundred pounds, were sprinting southwest along the summit. Running beside them was a much larger shimmermoth, its wing-like sensors flopping up and down with every galloping step. Infinity had never seen a shimmermoth run so fast, and it was rare to see one with a group of tiger beetles. The two predator species usually avoided each other.

She whipped around and scanned the scene below, a vast, moss-covered plain dotted with framework hills that resembled overturned teacups. The moss and hills looked strange in the light of the multi-colored aurora above and the steadily-rising sun in the east. The plain was now illuminated enough that she could make out groups of various arthropod species, both predators and moss grazers, fleeing toward the south.

The timing of all these bizarre events was too perfect to be a coincidence. Just yesterday afternoon, her old boss and friend Armando Doyle, along with a physicist and a handful of Marines, had miraculously bridged to this world wearing clothing and carrying weapons. This should have been impossible. Armando had promised to return today at noon to extract any of the colonists who wanted to leave. This had come unexpectedly. Infinity's tiny colony had been surviving on this world for over a year and a half. Now, only twelve hours after Armando's appearance, some weird atmospheric or geologic event was causing massive auroras and panicking the wildlife. No, it couldn't be just coincidence.

For all these months, Infinity had been trying to shut out her haunting memories of her own dying Earth. Now those memories came rushing back with a vengeance.

She grabbed her tunic and shorts, both made from isopod belly skin, and pulled them on. The clothes were now splattered with the goo of suicidal flying arthropods, but that hardly seemed important. She started down the hillside but only made it a few dozen steps before she heard a deep rumbling that seemed to be coming from the north. She stopped to listen. The hillside jerked abruptly beneath her, and she toppled onto the moss. She struggled to get to her hands and knees, but the ground kept shifting.

Loud cracking sounds erupted from different points around her, and sheets of fractured bedrock began sliding down the hill. Infinity launched herself upward just in time to avoid being crushed by one of the sheets that was at least twenty yards wide. She came down hard on the sliding sheet of rock and rolled to the side until she tumbled off its edge. She then steadied herself with outspread arms and legs and watched the rock sheet as it continued hurtling down the slope like a colossal sled, gouging out massive amounts of moss and soil as it built momentum. The rock was sliding directly toward the framework mound her colony had painstakingly converted into a multi-unit residence—it was going to destroy Mossview.

She got to her knees and screamed, "Desmond! Gideon! Get everyone out!" But the roar of the heaving ground drowned out her voice completely.

The rock slab leveled out at the base of the hill and kept sliding. It slammed into Mossview's base, breaking through the framework of girders as if they were made of paper. It came to a stop with only a few yards of its bulk still protruding from the mound.

"Desmond!" Infinity cried as she got to her feet. With the ground still shaking, she sprinted down the slope but then fell again near the base of the hill. As she was getting up, she saw the colony's livestock—dog-sized hermit crabs and half-grown, thousand-pound isopods—crashing through their enclosures and scattering in panic. The colonists began emerging from Mossview. Infinity started running toward the structure, counting people as they came out. At least eight, including one of the kids, Lenny and Isabelle's daughter Daisy. But Desmond wasn't with them. "Desmond!" she cried again.

Four more had emerged by the time she reached the group. Desmond and six others were still unaccounted for. She dashed past the colonists and ducked through the doorway. "Desmond!"

"Over here, Infinity. You okay?"

"I'm fine." She made her way through a corridor paneled with eight-foot sections of isopod carapace and entered the central chamber where the colonists gathered for meals. It was still dark in here, with only minimal light coming through the smoke vent at the mound's peak. "Where are you?"

"Here! I'm okay too, but we've got a problem."

She muttered a curse. He was in the section of Mossview nearest the hillside, which probably meant someone had been hurt by the sliding rock. Otherwise he would have cleared everyone out by now. She entered another corridor and made it about ten yards in before her path was blocked by collapsed framework girders and the edge of the sheet of rock. Apparently the rock had completely destroyed the largest apartment in Mossview, where Àurea, Sarah, Tyrone, and their six-month-old boy Brooks slept. Infinity peered through the gaps between the girders and saw Desmond to her right, crouching by the edge of the slab. She continued searching and found the two National Guardsmen, Gideon Stead and Steven Irizar, to her left.

"I don't see any sign of them," Desmond said.

"Nothing here either," Gideon reported.

Steven said, "Maybe they got out ahead of us."

Infinity noticed a dark red puddle seeping out from beneath the rock, creeping toward the shattered pieces of framework girder at her feet. For a moment she simply stared, hesitant to speak up in case the puddle wasn't actually what it appeared to be. The red liquid rippled slightly as the ground continued shaking. Reluctantly, she touched the puddle and then smelled her finger—definitely blood. "One of them is beneath this rock, maybe more," she said. "And I didn't see any of them outside." The words came out as if she were simply making an observation about the weather, rather than reporting that four members of her close-knit colonist family had been crushed to death by tons of solid rock.

Desmond, Gideon, and Steven made their way toward her, ducking through openings in the framework and stepping over broken pieces until they were standing at her side.

Gideon silently kneeled by the pooling blood and stared at it. He leaned closer to the two-inch gap between the rock and the ground. "Tyrone! Sarah! Can anyone hear me?"

Nothing. Gideon tried again. Still no answer. He stood up. "Jesus Christ, what the hell's happening?"

The ground started trembling harder, as if in response.

Infinity just kept staring at the expanding pool of blood, trying not to think about the possibility that it was from baby Brooks. Finally, she pulled her eyes away. "I don't know, but it's major. The animals are going nuts out there. And before the quakes started, an aurora filled the entire sky."

Desmond stared at her. "What?"

She shook her head slightly. "I've got a really bad feeling about this."

Shouts from the colonists outside rose above the rumble. Gideon and Steven started moving toward the front doorway.

"Come on," Desmond said. "We have to get away from the hillside before more rocks come down."

Infinity tore her gaze away from the blood one more time and then turned to go. As she took her first step, the ground beneath Mossview heaved, throwing her upward. She hit her head on one of the girders, and then she and Desmond fell to the ground in a heap. The massive rock sheet, which had also been thrown upward, crashed back to the ground with a stomach-wrenching thud. The air filled with cracking and rattling sounds as the framework above Mossview's central chamber collapsed. Hundreds of girder shards came crashing down, filling up the chamber and blocking the path to the front door.

Desmond got to his feet and pulled Infinity up. "This way!" he shouted. He climbed onto the rock slab and started crawling toward the opening the rock had created. Infinity scrambled onto the slab and followed just behind him.

As they emerged from what was left of Mossview's structure, Infinity looked up at the hillside. An even larger sheet of rock was sliding directly at them. "Shit, look out!" she cried.

She and Desmond lunged to the side and jumped to the

ground just as the second rock slammed into the first, shoving it even farther into Mossview. The entire mound collapsed, sending razor-sharp girder pieces flying in all directions. One piece caught Infinity's shoulder, sending a shockwave of pain down her arm. She crouched and raised her arms to shield her face. She glanced at her shoulder. Luckily, the shard hadn't cut through her tunic.

More rock slabs and boulders were sliding and tumbling down the hillside.

She grabbed Desmond's arm. "Come on!"

They started running away from the hillside along the perimeter of Mossview's rubble, stumbling every few steps as the massive quake's aftershocks rumbled on. Infinity could see the other colonists several hundred yards ahead steadily making their way to the northeast, trying to put some distance between themselves and the deadly rocks.

To the northeast, another framework mound collapsed, this one at least twice the size of Mossview.

The other colonists stopped once they had put about a quarter mile between themselves and the hillside, and Desmond and Infinity quickly caught up with them. She counted fourteen people besides herself and Desmond, which meant that Àurea, Sarah, Tyrone, and baby Brooks were definitely gone.

For several long minutes, nobody spoke as they all tried to stay on their feet. Infinity watched the hillside for dislodged boulders that might roll out this far.

"What in God's name is happening?" Hayley Millwright asked. Hayley had once been the President of the United States, before the group's own version of Earth had been destroyed. Her husband, Alexander, had lost most of his right leg shortly after bridging to this world, and she and their daughter Isabelle were now standing next to him, helping to stabilize him.

Poppy Safran, one of the colony's med techs, pointed to the east. "Oh crap. Everyone brace yourselves!"

Infinity turned just in time to see a wave approaching. But it wasn't water. It was the ground itself, buckling violently, toppling framework hills and throwing rocks and soil into the air. There was no time to respond—the wave was upon them.

Infinity grabbed Desmond's elbow just before the ground beneath them heaved and threw the colonists several feet into the air like rag dolls. They all hit the ground in a screaming, flailing pile. Infinity got to her hands and knees and watched the wave continue speeding west. It hit Mossview's remains, scattering the already-destroyed structure into an unrecognizable jumble, and then it ran into the hillside. The entire hill shuddered, shaking loose impossibly large expanses of rock, which began sliding and tumbling down the slope.

Infinity got to her feet. "We're still too close to the hillside. We have to go!" She helped Lenny to his feet. He was still holding baby Daisy in his arms. The little girl's eyes were wide, but oddly she wasn't crying. Gideon and Steven took over helping Alexander, and the group started moving away from the hillside as quickly as the trembling ground would allow.

Infinity looked back over her shoulder. Most of the flat sheets of bedrock were coming to a stop at the base of the hill, but dozens of irregular pieces were continuing to roll and bounce across the moss. A boulder the size of a small house was tumbling directly toward the fleeing group. "Everyone stop!" she cried. Two other smaller boulders were approaching on the left, so she grabbed Desmond's hand and began pulling him to the right. "This way—move it!"

The boulder crashed by just behind them, each impact gouging the earth and vibrating Infinity's bones.

"Oh my God, things are about to get worse," said Reece Eagleton. Reece was the FEMA administrator who had overseen SafeTrek Bridging's attempts to evacuate human colonies in the days leading up to Earth's collapse. Reece was now pointing to a rising column of debris to the east. The plume was miles away, and it had to be at least half a mile tall.

Infinity watched as the outer edges of the dark cloud began falling slowly back toward the ground. The plume wasn't smoke at all—it was dirt and rocks. She stared in disbelief. What kind of force could possibly blast that much solid material half a mile into the sky? She noticed a deep roar coming from the direction of the plume, growing louder by the second.

"We have to get to the bridge-in site," Desmond said.

Infinity turned to him. He was right. The entire planet was tearing itself apart, and soon no place would be safe. They had to get off this world.

"But Doyle and the others aren't coming for us until noon," said Eagleton.

Infinity frowned at him. "Maybe they'll come early. If you have a better idea, spit it out."

Eagleton shook his head. "I'm not disagreeing, just stating facts. They're coming at noon. Not only that, but the bridge-in site is three miles away."

Infinity glanced at the debris cloud again. "Then we'd better move our asses."

2

———

WAVES

APRIL 10 - MORNING

DESMOND WEAVER HAD CONSIDERED himself lucky. After all, he was one of the few survivors of his species. But now his luck had run out. He was witnessing—for the second time—what appeared to be the destruction of an entire world.

The group he had been living with for the last nineteen months was still reeling from the tragic loss of four of their fellow colonists. Now they were down to only sixteen. He and Infinity were leading the survivors northwest, toward the bridge-in site. If they made it there alive, they would still have to stay safe long enough for Armando Doyle to bridge in and then somehow bridge the entire colony out. Which Desmond had thought was physically impossible until Armando had unexpectedly appeared yesterday.

So far, the group had traveled perhaps a mile, but progress had been slow because they frequently had to steady themselves against violent tremors and occasional seismic surface waves that buckled the ground and destroyed every framework hill in their path. Desmond's observations over the last year and a half had led him to conclude that these framework hills were probably thousands of years old, created gradually by the secretions of a specific type of moss that lived atop the girders. But now every one of these once-magnificent structures, stretching as far as he could see, lay in ruins.

Infinity nudged his arm and nodded toward the west. "Another one."

He followed her gaze. Perhaps ten miles away, a massive spire of rocks and dirt was flying straight up, the explosive result of a volcano or some other cataclysm. If such an event were to occur within a mile or two of the group's location, the colonists would no doubt be buried in falling debris or swallowed by fissures in the ground.

Desmond scanned the horizon for other eruptions, and his gaze lingered on another cloud, this one only about a half mile away. At first it appeared to be smoke, but he had spent enough time on this world to recognize that it was a swarm of the remarkable hive creatures that lived here. In fact, based on the location, the billions of flies making up this cloud were probably the collective intelligence he knew as Laghollow. As bizarre as it seemed, he had become friends with this hive mind, as well as several others. But now Laghollow's home, a framework mound, had almost certainly been destroyed along with all the other mounds. Desmond wondered if the hive minds would perish.

Fortunately, the route to the bridge-in site didn't require them to traverse any major hills—just the moss plain. With the framework mounds already destroyed, the colonists wouldn't have to worry about falling rocks or debris as they made their way to the northwest. All they had to do was get to the site and stay alive until Armando showed up.

After the group had traveled another half mile or so, they encountered an obstacle—a herd of isopods moving steadily west as quickly as the hippo-sized creatures could walk. But this wasn't like the isopod herds Desmond was used to seeing, which typically numbered thirty to fifty. This was a continuous stream of them, perhaps forty yards wide, with no end in sight to the east or west. The creatures were walking so close together they were constantly bumping into each other.

The colonists stood staring at the impenetrable wall of biomass for a few minutes. Eventually, Lenny said, "I can't believe I'm saying this, but hell, we have to go through them." Lenny was still carrying Daisy, and the little ten-month-old was somehow sleeping in his arms.

"We can't," said Isabelle. "Look at them. They're panicked. They'll crush us."

She was right, they were panicked. But even so, they were walking no faster than the average human could walk. Still, the creatures weighed at least a ton each. The thought of Lenny carrying Daisy through the herd made Desmond's stomach lurch.

"Lenny's right," Infinity said. "We have to get to the bridge-in site, and this herd isn't going to pass by any time soon." She stepped forward and proceeded to the nearest lumbering beast. She then leaned into its side while keeping pace with it. The creature's fourteen legs scuffled for a moment as it shifted direction slightly, but then it bumped into the isopod next to it and went back to its original path. Isopods were generally docile animals, but this panicked herd was too densely arranged for the colonists to be able to clear a path.

"Look," Lenny said, "I've hunted these lumbering oafs long enough to know they won't run over us."

Desmond eyed Lenny, a friend he had known and trusted

since long before their version of Earth had collapsed. "You sure about that?"

Xavier, another long-time friend of Desmond's, had been standing next to his partner Celia, but now he stepped forward and spoke to Lenny. "Dude, you need to be really sure." He nodded toward Celia's bulging belly. She was six months pregnant, and everyone in this colony understood how precious each new life was.

Lenny smiled, a strange gesture under the circumstances, even for him. "Watch and learn," he said. Still cradling Daisy in his arms, he approached the edge of the herd, waited for a gap to appear, and then stepped directly into the path of one of the isopods. The creature's antennae, each as thick as a human arm, tapped Lenny's ankles, and the isopod stopped abruptly, which halted the isopod behind it, as well as the one behind that one. After the beasts had paused for only a few seconds, they changed course and skirted around Lenny and Daisy.

Lenny turned back to Isabelle and smiled, apparently to reassure her. He then carried his daughter deeper into the herd until he was blocking the path of yet another isopod, causing the creature and those behind it to change course slightly. He looked back at the colonists and smiled again. He was now completely surrounded by the massive, shoulder-high isopods, with only his head still visible. "The trick is to not let them intimidate you," he called out over the tectonic rumblings and the scraping, shuffling sounds of the herd.

The colonists glanced at each other nervously.

"Let's do this," Infinity said. "We need to get to the site—we have no other option."

As if to emphasize her point, a new roar rose above all the other sounds. The group turned and saw a plume of the planet's crust shooting skyward a few miles to the east.

"Alright, everybody listen," said Desmond, almost shouting to be heard. "Celia and Chloe are pregnant, so we need to form a circle around them so they don't get knocked over by the isopods."

Celia looked like she was about to protest, but then she and Chloe nodded and moved into place.

"We'll all stay together as a group," Desmond said. "Like we're one large animal. We want to give the isopods every possible reason to go around us."

"You coming or not?" Lenny was now at the center of the river of monstrous bugs.

The others tightened their formation, crowding around the two pregnant women. Gideon and Steven were still helping Alexander, and the three of them positioned themselves at the rear.

"Move slowly, but also with confidence," Infinity said as she pushed Richard and Poppy closer into the group. "Now, follow our lead."

She and Desmond began backing toward the herd and encouraging the group to follow.

At the herd's edge, Desmond's heart began pounding. What if bunching up like this was a mistake? Maybe they should split up and enter the herd one at a time.

He was about to voice his rising concerns, but then Infinity stepped into a gap between isopods, and the rest of the group followed. Two of the isopods detected the humans' presence and paused, creating a traffic jam behind them. But the creatures quickly adjusted their path and began walking around the group, snuffling the ground with their low-slung heads and rhythmically moving their numerous feet.

Desmond's eyes met Infinity's, and he nodded, trying to appear more confident than he felt.

She nodded back and turned to wait for another opening.

A few seconds later, she guided the group into another gap, with the same result—the isopods paused and then detoured. The colonists continued making steady progress with only minor jostling from the passing beasts.

"You're almost through!" Lenny shouted. He was now clear of the herd, standing on the other side with Daisy still sleeping in his arms. Suddenly, he snapped his head toward the east and said, "Oh, shit!"

Desmond started to turn and look, but then he was nearly knocked off his feet by a ground tremor. Several of the other colonists fell to their knees. The entire isopod herd stopped walking, as if bracing for another shockwave. Once Desmond had regained his balance, he looked out to the east and felt his jaw drop. Just as his mind was beginning to comprehend the immense scale of the new rising cloud of debris, the sound wave arrived, drowning out every other sound with its gut-clenching roar.

The isopods began moving again, this time even more panicked than before. One of them jostled the group of humans from the side and knocked everyone to the ground. But the giants still appeared to be altering their course as their antennae detected the writhing pile of humans. Desmond pushed himself up and got to his feet, all the while fighting the urge to shield his ears from the deafening onslaught of sound.

He needed to help the others get up, but his eyes were drawn to the east. This new eruption was less than a mile away, and the wall of rising debris seemed impossibly high. Yet it was getting higher and wider by the second. He squinted at the cloud. Among the rising specks he could make out boulders and chunks of blasted earth, but there was some-thing else—hundreds of dots, all of them uniform in size. He swallowed as he realized what he was looking at. The dots were isopods. The explosion had occurred directly beneath the herd. The cloud was expanding. Isopods and chunks of rock and soil were flying out in every direction.

Desmond shook off his stupor. "Get up now!" he screamed at the others. But it was no use—they couldn't hear him over the noise. He saw that Infinity was helping the colonists get to their feet, and he joined in the effort, grabbing elbows and hoisting people up.

The isopods surrounding the colonists were now spreading out, abandoning their tight formation, apparently due to their renewed agitation.

Steven took over the job of assisting Alexander, and Gideon joined Desmond and Infinity as they prodded the colonists through the herd until they were beside Lenny. Daisy was crying now, although Desmond could barely hear her over the constant rumble.

Infinity pointed up at the expanding plume and yelled something unintelligible.

Desmond glanced upward. It was now clear that the cloud was going to expand far enough that the debris would soon start raining down on the colonists. The plume was far too expansive for them to have any hope of getting out of its way.

Someone shook Desmond's shoulder, and he pulled his eyes from the horror above. It was Infinity. She yanked him closer and shouted in his ear. "No way to outrun it! Tell the others to spread out. Tell them to watch the falling debris and be ready to move out of the way!"

She pulled back and glared into his eyes. He nodded. She then moved to Gideon and started yelling in his ear, presumably giving the same instructions.

Desmond stepped over to Xavier, filled him in on the plan, and told him to help spread the word. One by one, they communicated the instructions to the rest of the group, although some of the colonists shook their heads, apparently not liking the idea of separating. But Infinity's reasoning was sound. As one of the few remaining colonies of surviving humans from Earth, they couldn't risk losing everyone at once.

The group reluctantly began spreading out. Infinity waved for them to continue moving apart even farther, until they were all at least twenty yards from each other.

Desmond positioned himself as near to Infinity as he thought she would allow and then turned toward the sky. Although chunks of earth were still spewing upward from the source of the volcanic energy, the outer debris was now on its way to the ground after having been propelled well over a half mile into the sky.

Desmond's adrenaline was in full surge, and his muscles were tight. He scanned the area and saw that Hayley and Alexander Millwright were huddled together on the ground with their arms covering their heads. Why weren't they watching the sky? At this point there was no way to get their attention. He looked over at Infinity. She met his gaze and then pressed two fingers to her eyes and pointed upward, signaling for him to watch the sky.

Desmond took a deep breath and turned his gaze skyward. A massive field of falling debris was now only a few hundred yards above him. It was still too soon to tell whether anything was headed straight toward him, so he simply stood in place. Several seconds later, he spotted a massive incoming object. He darted to his left. A two-thousand-pound isopod struck the ground where he'd been standing and exploded. A piece of carapace glanced off his shoulder and knocked him down. Lying on his back, he guarded his head with his arms and watched as debris rained down around him. Most of the objects were small. The few boulders and additional isopods he could see were falling to the east, closer to the initial eruption. After about thirty seconds he decided it was safe to get up and take his eyes off the sky.

Most of the other colonists were still on their feet and appeared to be unhurt. Hayley and Alexander were still huddling together with their faces down, and Desmond ran over to them. Unable to speak to them due to the constant roar, he put a hand on each of the Millwrights' shoulders and shook them. They uncovered their heads and looked up, apparently unharmed. Desmond and Hayley helped Alexander get up and stand on his one leg.

Desmond scanned the sky once more for falling debris and then counted the colonists. Everyone was there. Emily Sanchez, one of the guardsmen, was holding a hand over a bleeding wound on the back of her head, but when Desmond pointed at her she nodded, indicating she was okay.

Infinity made her way over to Desmond and leaned close to his ear. "Have to keep moving. Bridge-in site. Now!"

He nodded and they both waved for the others to follow. They all began making their way northwest with renewed urgency.

The next mile or so of their journey was punctuated by numerous tremors and ground swells knocking the colonists off their feet, but finally the group found themselves approaching the bridge-in site. Desmond had begun to worry that they wouldn't be able to find the site. With the framework mounds reduced to rubble, the once-familiar terrain now looked like an alien landscape. But then Infinity pointed, having spotted something ahead. She was pointing at a symmetrical object about a quarter mile away. It appeared to be a green cone with its narrow end pointing toward the sky. Tubular ribs—or perhaps pipes—were arranged vertically around the curved exterior, converging at the cone's tip.

Desmond turned to Infinity, and she shook her head and

shrugged. Desmond's best guess was that the object was something Armando intended to use for bridging the colonists off this world. Considering he had previously thought such a feat to be impossible, why should he be surprised that some bizarre piece of equipment was needed? Perhaps it was even a portable bridging device, constructed entirely out of bridge-able organic components.

The constant roar of distant eruptions was still loud enough to make conversation impossible, so the colonists began stumbling their way toward the green cone. As they approached the structure, Desmond realized it was larger than he had estimated from a distance, standing at least thirty feet tall. Its surface was uniformly forest green, with no features except for fifteen or so evenly-spaced cylindrical pipes or conduits running from bottom to top. Armando and the Marines were nowhere to be seen, which wasn't surprising since the colonists had arrived at least an hour early, by Desmond's estimation. Considering the planet seemed to be self-destructing, and at an alarming rate, even an hour was far too long to wait.

Infinity nudged Desmond's arm and pointed east. He followed her gaze to the nearest collapsed framework hill. Scurrying aimlessly around the jumbled pile of girders were hundreds of skitterbugs, the green, lobster-sized creatures that had once inhabited the mound. In fact, it was probably the same swarm that had attacked the human refugees minutes after they had originally bridged to this world over eighteen months ago. One of the refugees, a historian named William, had disappeared during the attack, never to be seen again. No one knew for sure, but everyone assumed the skitterbugs had eaten him. Desmond felt no pity for the now-homeless creatures.

The colonists had nothing to do but wait. That, and hope

Armando would show up before they were all crushed by falling debris or blasted a half mile into the sky by an eruption beneath their feet. Most of the colonists stood staring out at the now-countless distant eruptions, while Desmond walked around the green cone, looking for clues as to its purpose. He saw no visible hatches or control panels—no way to get inside. He rapped his knuckles on the surface. As he had expected, it was hard, but the background noise made it impossible to hear whether it sounded hollow or solid. He pressed an ear to it. He couldn't be sure, but he thought he heard humming resonating from within. Whatever the object was, it seemed to be doing something.

As Desmond finished making his way around the cone and returned to his original position, a group of figures appeared out of thin air about thirty yards away. They were all men in black fatigues, the Marines who had accompanied Armando the previous evening. The men teetered for only a few seconds before regaining their balance. Their eyes widened as they took in the huge columns of blasted material in the distance. Several of the dozen or so men instinctively covered their ears against the assault of noise, releasing their weapons to hang loosely on the slings around their necks and shoulders.

The men glanced around until they spotted the waiting colonists. They started making their way over, but their eyes were drawn to the green cone. They exchanged frowns and puzzled glances.

Desmond approached them, and one of the men stepped forward cautiously, obviously struggling to keep his balance with the ground shaking beneath his feet. Desmond leaned closer and shouted in the Marine's ear, "We have to go, now!"

"What the hell is happening?" the Marine shouted back. He then pulled back before Desmond could answer and simply nodded, apparently deciding he didn't need details at this time. He motioned to the other men, and one of them stepped forward with what appeared to be a leather bag. The first man took the bag, opened it, and pulled out a handful of oblong, glistening pellets that vaguely resembled raw oysters. He leaned in to Desmond's ear and shouted, "Eat one! Radioisotope marker!"

Desmond nodded and took one of the pellets. The Marine then moved to the other colonists and started handing them out, motioning toward his mouth to indicate that they were to be eaten. The man shouted in Lenny's ear for a moment and then squeezed the juice from one of the pellets into Daisy's mouth.

Desmond popped his own pellet into his mouth, chewed it, and swallowed. It had been flavored with vanilla extract, but it had the texture of a raw oyster. Perhaps it *was* a raw oyster, injected with Technetium-99m. This would be an ingenious way to make radioisotope doses bridgeable.

Technetium-99m was the radioisotope marker necessary for a bridging device to locate a person's body and pull the person back to the world they had bridged from. Desmond and the other colonists had bridged to this world without taking doses of the marker. At the time, they had believed that doing so would mean they would be stuck permanently on this version of Earth.

Desmond approached the man who had originally carried the bag of radioisotope doses. He briefly considered talking to the man by projecting his thoughts through physical contact, an ability he'd acquired nineteen months ago on another version of Earth. But he decided against it—this wasn't the time to hit these guys with something that might startle them or downright freak them out.

Instead, he yelled in the man's ear, "How long? It's not safe here!"

The man pulled back, tapped his wrist even though he had no watch, and held up three fingers.

Desmond mouthed the word, "Minutes?"

The guy nodded.

Desmond let out a sigh of relief. They were going to make it off this world alive. He tried to mouth the words "Thank you," but the guy was now staring to the east with a horrified look on his face. Desmond spun around. Something wasn't right. The landscape to the east had changed. A mountain range was now visible in the distance, whereas before there had been only an open moss plain all the way to the horizon. He realized suddenly that the mountain range was moving, getting closer. It wasn't a mountain range at all, but a wave, a buckling of the world's surface, unimaginably high and moving west, directly toward the bridge-in site.

Desmond could only stare, paralyzed by fear, as he struggled to wrap his mind around the enormity of the wave's destructive power. Everything in its path—hills, rivers, living creatures—would be heaved hundreds of yards into the air and crushed in the churning amalgam of bedrock and soil. It looked like the wave would reach them in less than thirty seconds.

The humans had to bridge out now or die.

Desmond shook off his shock and turned to see Infinity and several of the Marines frantically herding the colonists into a cluster around the spot where the men had bridged in. He joined in the effort, and seconds later the entire group was standing shoulder to shoulder. The Marine who had handed out the radioisotope pellets was now fumbling with a device he had pulled from his belt, but his hands were shaking with panic, causing him to drop the device. He pounded the side of his head in frustration, picked up the device, and glanced to the east before trying again.

Desmond turned and stared at the approaching tsunami of earth and rock, unable to even guess at its height. The closer the wave got, the faster it appeared to be moving. It would be upon them in seconds. He felt Infinity put her arms around him from behind. She knew. She knew they weren't going to make it. He put both his hands on her arms and squeezed.

The wave was towering over them so tall he had to crane his neck to see its crest. It was the most beautiful yet the most terrifying sight he'd ever seen. Splotches of green, brown, and gray blinked in and out of sight as swaths of moss, rock, and soil roiled violently on the wave's surface. It occurred to him that the level of noise now was no louder than before, and then he realized the wave had to be traveling faster than the speed of sound.

Desmond felt the ground begin to rise beneath his feet. He wanted to close his eyes but couldn't stop staring at the force that was about to kill him and everyone he cared about.

A voice to his right, barely audible, screamed, "Yes! Yes!"

Everything suddenly became silent, except for Daisy's crying.

3

———

RHF

April 10 - 11:31 AM

INFINITY REALIZED she was still gripping Desmond tightly around his waist. She released him and pulled back. She was now standing on a padded floor in a white room. Her adrenaline was still flowing, causing her muscles to twitch as if coaxing her to run or fight. But there was nothing here to fight, nothing to run from. She and the other colonists were standing in a bridging chamber, similar to SafeTrek's but larger by at least half.

She glanced down at her own body. Her isopod-skin clothes and shoes were gone. She ran her fingers over her scalp. The shoulder-length hair she'd been growing for the last nineteen months was also gone. The other refugees around her were similarly hairless and naked. But the dozen or so Marines were still fully-clothed and armed with their strange weapons that were apparently made of living tissue. One of the Marines immediately removed his helmet, revealing that he was bald like everyone else.

"That was unexpectedly brief," said Armando's voice over the comm system. "And it appears you convinced others of your group to come with you, Infinity. What a pleasant surprise!"

Infinity turned and saw a viewing window in the chamber's wall to her right. Armando was on the other side, along with the physicist Kyle Fornas, who had been with Armando the previous evening.

"We encountered unexpected complications," said one of the Marines.

A staggering understatement.

Infinity stepped forward. "Armando, our world—our home—was in the process of self-destructing. It started just a few hours ago. There's no way in hell it wasn't somehow related to you bridging in last night."

Armando's eyes widened, showing genuine surprise. "Self-destructing? How?"

"Just like our own version of Earth, only much faster. It started just this morning, and we were lucky to bridge out alive."

"There was something there, sir, at the bridge-in site," said the Marine who had handed out doses of radioisotope to the colonists. "It was a piece of machinery. Big as a house. Never seen anything like it."

Armando frowned and shook his head. "There wasn't anything like that at the bridge-in site yesterday. How did it get there?"

"I was hoping you could tell me," said the Marine. The guy was understandably rattled, and his tone hinted at suspicion.

Armando shook his head. "This is all very confusing."

"It's also quite alarming," said the scientist beside him. "I had been under the impression that the key discovered by your people revealed all that we needed to know in order to use bridging technology safely. We must stop activating the device immediately, before we cause irreparable damage to the planet. Assuming we haven't done so already."

"I'd like to get out of these clothes," said one of the Marines. "They feel like they're made out of live weasels. Can someone open the hatch?"

Infinity took a closer look at the nearest Marine's fatigues. The material didn't look anything like live weasels, but it did kind of resemble the skin of a black lizard.

The hatch popped open. Several techs in white bio-suits stepped through and gestured for the Marines to exit the chamber. Infinity started to step toward the hatch, but one of the techs put out a gloved hand to stop her. "You'll be allowed through the hatch in a moment, ma'am."

She turned and raised a brow at Armando.

"They have their own protocols, Infinity," he said. "Keep in mind that this world has been on a different timeline from our own for over twenty-one years." He gave a sidelong glance at the physicist beside him. "They've been kind to us, but there are differences, as you'll soon see."

After the Marines had exited the chamber, three more techs in bio-suits entered the chamber, and one of them, a woman who appeared to be in her fifties, addressed the refugees. "I'm Dr. Trini Soloman. First, I'd like to welcome you to our Earth, and to the National Bridging Center. I'd also like to express my sympathy regarding the destruction of your own Earth nearly two years ago. Although we haven't experienced anything so devastating as that, it is important for you to be aware that our world has faced its own unique challenges. In the nearly twenty-two years since your universe diverged from ours, we have endured a devastating pandemic, from a disease known as RHF—red howler fever. It has changed the very fabric of our country, making us particularly cautious. We'll examine each of you more carefully in the adjoining medical labs, but I'm afraid we must insist on performing a cursory skin exam before we can even allow you out of the bridging chamber. It won't take long, I assure you."

"Ma'am," Lenny said, "after saving us from the zip-banging shitstorm we just went through, you're welcome to probe every crack and orifice if that tickles your fancy. We're just freaking grateful to be in one piece."

Dr. Soloman forced a slight smile behind her bio-suit face-plate. "Red howler fever presents as scaly skin rashes. As soon as we've verified that none of you are displaying symptoms, you'll be able to leave the chamber."

Infinity wondered what these people would do if any of the refugees did happen to have a rash. Would they simply seal the hatch and bridge the entire group to another world?

The techs spread out and began examining the newcomers. One of the techs, a guy who looked younger than Infinity, came directly to her and began shining what appeared to be an ultraviolet light at her skin. He was very thorough, illuminating and examining every square inch, starting with her face and scalp. As he worked his way down her body, Infinity gazed at the walls and ceiling of the bridging chamber. During the last nineteen months she had become accustomed to living in a crudely-constructed dwelling and seeing nothing but natural objects, plants, and living creatures. It was almost discomforting to be in a sterile, human-made structure, with smooth, flawless surfaces.

The tech moved his light down to her chest and said, "Lift your breasts, please."

She sighed and lifted them. At least the guy had the decency to keep his hands off her.

"What's the story with this red howler fever?" she asked.

The tech's eyes flicked to hers and he shook his head slightly. "Started fifteen years ago. An unknown virus. We had no warning. Patient zero was an American tourist returning from Venezuela. Turns out the guy had come across a dead red howler monkey, probably killed by a poacher or by other howlers in a territorial dispute. Anyway, the guy picks it up, has his picture taken with it. He comes back to the US. A week later, he gets a rash. A month after that, he's dead. By the time they figured out it was contagious, it was too late. The virus had already started spreading. It took seven years to finally get it under control, and by that point it had killed almost sixty-two million people."

"Sixty-two million?"

He looked at her through his faceplate. "Every single death has been in the United States. A pandemic like that tends to change the way other countries treat you. Americans aren't allowed to travel beyond our own borders. Not even to Mexico or Canada. Both countries have constructed border walls to keep us out. The quality of life here isn't what it used to be, so everyone wants to leave, but there's no place that will take us." The guy dropped to his knees and started inspecting her groin and butt.

Once all the refugees had been subjected to this inspection, they were moved to the med lab, which, like the bridging chamber, was larger than SafeTrek's. As the med techs were taking blood samples and throat swabs, Armando and the physicist Kyle Fornas entered the lab. They weren't wearing bio-suits, which indicated they too were in quarantine, probably due to having bridged to the colonists' world the previous day.

Armando smiled and addressed the colonists. "I was planning to apologize for not having bridged to your world with the squad of Marines this morning, but from what I've heard, it was not a pleasant place to be, and my presence wouldn't have been helpful."

"You're lucky you weren't there," Desmond said as a med tech stuck a needle in his arm. "It was like being in hell."

"We've lost two home worlds in less than two years," said Lenny, still cradling his daughter in his arms. "How many freaking people can say that?"

Armando shook his head. "I'm afraid this changes everything. I had grand plans for using this enhanced bridging center to rescue the colonists we had evacuated from our own Earth. I was certain we had constructed a bridging device that could be used safely, without causing harm to this world or any other. Now what are we to do?"

"We certainly cannot activate the machine again," said Fornas. "It's too risky. Especially considering what happened to your own version of Earth. Our scientists will have to re-examine everything we thought we knew."

Armando sighed heavily. "Yes, I agree completely. But meanwhile, the several thousand remaining refugees from our own Earth could be suffering and dying. It's all terribly exasperating."

"But there may be nothing wrong with your bridging device at all," Desmond said. "Like we told you, some kind of large machine had somehow appeared at the bridge-in site after you bridged back yesterday. It seems pretty likely that device had something to do with the planet's collapse."

They all fell silent for a few long seconds.

"We don't know that for sure yet," Fornas said. "There are many unanswered questions. I know you're eager to rescue your people, but it seems highly unlikely we'll be allowed to use the device until we fully understand what we're dealing with."

Infinity could see where this was going. "Which I assume might take years?"

Fornas looked at her and nodded. "If not longer."

A FEW HOURS LATER, the refugees had been shown to their rooms, which were located at the opposite end of the quarantine area from where the Marines were being housed. The rooms were small, but they were spacious enough to accommodate couples, or even a small family in the case of Lenny, Isabelle, and Daisy.

The med techs had already examined everyone thoroughly, but Infinity had decided to talk to each of the refugees to assess their mental state. They were all exhausted, and they were struggling with the tragedy of having lost the home they'd made for themselves during the last nineteen months. They were all scared, with no idea what was going to happen to them next. Still, they were coping as well as could be expected.

Finally, Infinity and Desmond were alone in their room. They each unfolded the paper pants, tops, and booties that had been left on their bed and dressed themselves. The clothes weren't all that different from the sterile paper garments that had sometimes been used at SafeTrek. Compared to their usual clothing made from isopod leather, they felt scratchy and flimsy.

Desmond stretched out on the bed and immediately closed his eyes.

"You don't want to talk?" Infinity asked.

He opened his eyes. "We can talk if you want to. I'm just not sure what to say right now."

"Never mind. Get some rest."

He closed his eyes again. Infinity started pacing the room, trying to banish visions of the horrors she'd witnessed since meditating on the rocky hillside above Mossview before daybreak. She had come to love her new world of giant, multi-legged arthropods and cognizant hives of flies. She couldn't believe it was gone, all of it, completely destroyed.

Someone tapped lightly on the door. "Infinity? Desmond?"

She opened it and found Armando standing there with a laptop in one hand. She stood aside and waved him in.

Desmond sighed and sat up. "Armando, I haven't really thanked you yet for finding us and bridging us off that world. We'd have been dead if we'd remained there for even a few more seconds."

Armando frowned. "I sincerely hope that our efforts to retrieve you weren't the *cause* of the disaster." He hesitated for a moment and then continued. "I cannot adequately express how relieved I am to have you and the remaining members of your colony here. I bridged to this world all those months ago with nineteen other refugees from our Earth, but all of those people have long since scattered throughout the country to start new lives." He displayed a smile that seemed forced. "We were all celebrities for a few months. The people here had no idea alternate universes even existed. I mean, how could they, having not yet discovered the Outlanders' radio signal? But the media folks quickly began to lose interest, as they tend to do, and eventually my compatriots from our version of Earth dispersed to find places for themselves in our new home. Some of them, I'm sure, just needed to distance themselves from the people who reminded them of the home they'd lost. Others decided they wanted to meet the alternate versions of themselves. I, myself, did not have that option. The other Armando Doyle was a casualty of red howler fever during the peak years of the disease's grip on this country."

Armando placed the laptop on the bed. "I hope you don't mind—I took the liberty of doing a bit of digging." He eyed Desmond. "I'm afraid, Desmond, that you're in the same boat as I am. The Desmond Weaver of this world succumbed to red howler fever ten years ago."

Desmond blew out a long breath of air. After contemplating this for a few moments, he asked, "Did you happen to look up my mom? Do you know if she's alive?"

Armando shook his head. "I didn't think to do that. I'd be happy to, if you'd like." He nodded down toward the laptop. "If she's alive, I could arrange for you to speak to her."

Desmond glanced at Infinity. "I... I don't know. Maybe I need some time to think about that. It wouldn't really be her, would it?"

"Well, yes and no. Depends on how you look at it. Either way, it's hard to predict how it would affect her to meet the son she lost ten years ago." Armando shook his head. "If you decide you'd like me to look into it, just let me know."

Infinity stared at the laptop, and her stomach started to tighten. "Why'd you bring that computer in here?"

Armando leveled his gaze at her. "Because, kiddo, I have taken the liberty of setting up a video chat for you. I assumed you'd be okay with it."

Her stomach tightened even more. "A video chat with who?"

"Her name is Passerina. She was a little confused when I first contacted her. But she has been following the news enough over the last year and a half to understand the concept of bridging. She'd like to meet you."

Infinity glared at him. "You *assumed* I'd be okay with this?"

Armando's face remained impassive. "You're quite fortunate to have this option. Desmond and I do not." He nodded at the laptop on the bed. "May I? She's actually waiting as we speak."

Infinity turned to Desmond. He shrugged and said, "What could it hurt?"

She closed her eyes for a moment and inhaled deeply. She had lived through a lot of screwed-up days in her thirty-one years, but this one just might top them all. She took a seat on the bed beside the laptop, suddenly feeling self-conscious about her appearance. She ran a hand over her scalp and looked up at Armando. Yesterday he had been wearing a helmet like the ones the Marines had been wearing, but now she could see the top of his head. "You just bridged yesterday," she said. "How is it you still have your hair?"

Armando smiled and patted his head. "This hair isn't actually mine. I realized months ago when we started testing the bridging device that without hair I resemble a featherless turkey. So I had this made." He tugged on the hairpiece, lifting it off his head slightly to prove it was fake. He smiled again. "If I didn't know you better, kiddo, I'd say you were stalling."

She gritted her teeth and glared at the computer. "Fine, let's get this over with."

Armando kneeled by the bed and opened the laptop. The screen lit up immediately. "The digital technology on this world is quite fascinating, really," he said. "This computer's operating system has had twenty-one years to develop in a separate timeline, and these people have come up with some truly innovative interface conventions. It seems that being isolated from the rest of the world due to red howler fever had an influence on—"

"Armando," Infinity said. "You know I don't give a fistful of farts about computers. I'm tired. Let's do this if we're gonna do it."

He nodded. "Yes. Yes indeed." He turned the computer toward himself and tapped a few times on the screen with his finger. A few seconds later, he smiled broadly. "Mrs. Stroud! Thank you for your patience. We are now ready on this end, if you are ready there."

"I'm as ready as I can be," a nervous voice said through the laptop's tiny speakers.

"Very well. Then it's my pleasure to introduce you to Passerina Fowler. For the last six years, she's been known as Infinity." He turned the laptop toward her.

Infinity stared at the woman on the screen and frowned. Perhaps Armando had made a mistake. The woman staring back at her was strikingly beautiful. She was wearing makeup. Infinity had never worn makeup in her life. The woman's hair was brown and short, styled perfectly to frame her face. Infinity's hair, during the few times she'd given it a chance to grow out, had been blonde. And this woman had no scars or bruises —no splotches of dirt or grime or blood.

The woman smiled. "It really is you. I mean... you're me!"

Infinity still couldn't see it. This woman looked nothing like her. She looked like those women on the television, or in a magazine.

"Mr. Doyle has told me all about you," the woman said. "He says you're a real hero, that you've saved countless lives. I was kind of intimidated by the idea of meeting you. I've never done anything like that." She forced a brief laugh. "I mean, I have a fit when I break a fingernail!"

Infinity saw it now, in the woman's eyes. Her face was a little puffy, but the eyes—they were Infinity's own eyes.

"I have to admit," said the woman, "I'm feeling proud

right now. Proud to know that I might actually be capable of the amazing things you've done."

Infinity tried swallowing, but her mouth was too dry. "Your last name is Stroud?"

"Yes, I took my husband's last name." The woman turned and looked at something off screen. "Come on, honey. It's okay." Another figure appeared on the screen, a little boy, and the woman hoisted him onto her lap. The boy appeared to be about five years old. "I'd like you to meet my son Maslin," said the woman, looking down at her son. "Can you say hello, Maslin?"

Infinity realized she had stopped breathing, and she sucked in a lungful of air.

"Hi," Maslin said. "What happened to your hair?"

Passerina Stroud put her hand on the boy's shoulder. "Maslin, that's not polite."

Infinity smiled. Her eyes were starting to water, so she wiped them with her thumb.

"Sorry," Maslin said, looking at the screen. "I like your head that way. It makes you look strong. Mommy, you should make your head bald too."

The woman laughed nervously as she lowered the boy to the floor. "Maybe I will, sweetheart. You can go play now."

Maslin turned to the screen, only the top of his head visible. He raised a hand and waved. "Bye!"

"Bye, Maslin," said Infinity.

"I apologize," the woman said. "He's all boy."

Infinity nodded. There were things she wanted to know, but she was finding it hard to speak. Finally, she managed to say, "Do you mind if I ask some questions?"

"Of course not."

Infinity straightened and smoothed the top of her sterile paper shirt, unsure how much of it the woman could even see.

She didn't like feeling rough in the presence of this polished woman. Armando should have given her some time to comprehend the weight of this conversation before opening the damn laptop. "Our worlds diverged twenty-one years ago," Infinity said. "From that point on we were on different time-lines. Do you understand how that works?"

The woman nodded. "Yes. I've been following the developments regarding bridging technology."

"Right, well, about four years after our timelines diverged, I got tired of living at home, and I ran away. I never went back. Did you run away, too?"

The woman gazed at her thoughtfully. "I remember considering it. But I never acted on it. I lived at home with Mom and Dad until I moved to Tempe for college."

Infinity stared at her. "You went to college?"

"Yes. BA in accounting. I've been a stay-at-home mom since Maslin was born, though. He'll start school in the fall, and then I'll be going back to work."

An accountant? Infinity didn't even know what an accountant did. "Um, Mom and Dad—are they still alive?"

The woman smiled. "Yes. Red howler fever didn't hit Phoenix as hard as some other areas—they say because it's so dry here." She then frowned. "What about on your own Earth? I mean, before what happened to it. Were Mom and Dad still alive there? Were they able to bridge off the world with you?"

Infinity closed her eyes for a moment. She then opened them and shook her head. "I never returned home after I left at fourteen. I don't know if they were alive."

The woman furrowed her brows. What was going through her mind? Was she wondering how in the hell someone could leave home at fourteen and never even check in on her own parents? "I'm sorry," she said. "Isn't it amazing how differently our lives have turned out?"

"Yeah, I guess so. I can't really imagine—"

Someone knocked sharply. "Mr. Doyle!"

Desmond got up and opened the door. A tech wearing a bio-suit was standing there, his eyes wide and his rhythmic breathing fogging his faceplate.

"Mr. Doyle, we've got a situation in the bridging chamber! Dr. Fornas says you need to come immediately. All three of you, actually. It's urgent."

Infinity turned back to the computer. "Sorry, I have to go."

The woman was frowning. "Is everything okay?"

"I don't know," said Infinity. "Something's come up." Armando reached over to shut the laptop, but Infinity grabbed his hand to stop him. "It was nice meeting you. Maybe we can talk again soon."

"Okay. Yes, it was nice. Thank you for—"

Armando shut the laptop and tucked it under his arm. They all followed the tech out of the room, through the main med lab, and into the bridging chamber viewing room. They weaved their way past several more bio-suited techs and joined Fornas in front of the viewing window.

Infinity stared into the chamber. Beyond the window, two men and a woman were staring back at her. All three of them had human-like faces, but the rest of their bodies suggested they were not human at all.

4

———————

STRANGERS

APRIL 10 - 4:13 PM

DESMOND STARED at the three beings in the bridging chamber. He had no doubt that they were intelligent. One glance told him that. He could see it not only in the way they looked back at him inquisitively, but also in their striking body ornamentation and grooming. They were nearly human in structure, except that black fur covered the creatures' entire bodies, fine and short like that of a Labrador retriever puppy. Portions of the fur were dyed with various colors, arranged in symmetrical patterns that tended to emphasize the beings' sturdy muscularity.

The creatures were nude except for minimalist rope-like garments worn around their waists, barely covering their genitals. These garments appeared to be made of dyed leather, and each being's was of a different design. One of the creatures was clearly a female, with firm-looking breasts much larger than those on the males. Her breasts were completely covered in fur except for the nipples.

Desmond's eyes were drawn back to the strangers' faces. All three of them were standing motionless, staring through the viewing window at the confused humans. At first, Desmond thought their faces were hairless, but when he looked more closely, he noticed a velvety sheen of fine hairs covering even their noses and the skin around their eyes. As with humans, the hair on their scalps was longer, but it was trimmed neatly to a length of about an inch. Each of the creatures had a distinctive pattern dyed into their scalp hair, complementing the dye patterns on the rest of their body.

The beings' faces were slightly broader than most human faces. Moreover, their entire bodies were stockier, with broader shoulders and stronger-looking arms. The female was slightly shorter than the two males but just as muscular.

"How did they get here?" Armando said, breaking the silence.

It seemed obvious to Desmond that the creatures had bridged in, although he had no idea how. Also, where did they come from? And what did they want?

"Have you ever had anyone bridge into this chamber like this before?" Infinity asked.

"Absolutely not," Fornas replied. "They must have bridged here from another version of Earth that has a bridging device in this same location."

"That's very unlikely," Armando said. "This facility has only been here a few months. The SafeTrek facility on our own version of Earth had only existed in this location for six years. That means that these people would have to have bridged from a world that diverged from ours less than six years ago. I don't see how people so strikingly different from us could have evolved in only six years."

The female on the other side of the window turned to the two males and started speaking to them.

"Can you turn on the comm system so we can hear them?" Desmond asked.

Fornas pressed a button on the wall. A voice came over the comm abruptly as one of the males responded to the female. His voice was higher-pitched than Desmond had expected based on the thickness of his body, but it still sounded very human. The language was completely foreign, though, and spoken at such a fast pace that Desmond probably wouldn't have been able to catch the meaning even if the creature had been speaking English.

The female spoke again, apparently cutting the male off, her words blasting out like a recording on triple speed.

"This is most fascinating!" Armando exclaimed.

All at once, the three beings looked up at the speaker in the bridging chamber ceiling. One of the males turned to the humans, and he actually appeared to be smiling. He held up his arm and pointed to a device strapped to his forearm. He then gestured to his mouth and spit out a rapid sequence of words while doing a rolling motion near his mouth with his hand.

"He wants us to keep speaking," Desmond said.

The creature heard this and his smile broadened. He rolled his hand near his mouth again.

"Do you understand what we're saying?" asked Dr. Fornas.

The male showed no signs of understanding, but he kept beckoning them to continue speaking. He pointed again at the device on his arm. The gadget was about six inches long and three inches wide, with four blocky segments of varying thicknesses. Desmond then noticed that each of the three strangers had one of these devices strapped to their left arm, and all three devices were forest green in color.

"You want us to keep speaking to you, don't you?" Desmond asked, looking directly at the male who had been gesturing. "You want us to speak because you're analyzing our speech. The more we speak, the more your devices learn to translate. You want to be able to speak back to us."

The man put a finger to his device and pressed something. A voice came from the device. "You... speak." The voice was a simulation of Desmond's own voice.

"Okay, yes, I will speak to you," Desmond said. "We will all speak to you." He turned to the others in the viewing room, all of whom were eyeing him with perplexed looks. "I think we should do it—we should each talk a bit, one at a time," he said. "It probably doesn't matter much what you say. Tell a story, explain your theory of the meaning of life, recite a poem. The more you say, the better their devices will be able to translate English. Do you mind if I begin?"

Fornas simply nodded, still looking perplexed.

Desmond turned back to the three beings. "My friends and I welcome you to this world. I should explain that I've had a very bad day. This morning, the world I had been living on for the past year and a half began to self-destruct. The structure we had modified to be our living quarters was destroyed by large rocks shaken loose by an earthquake. During the destruction, four of my friends were killed, including a young child."

He proceeded to explain the rest of the day's events, including their narrow escape from the collapsing planet and what they had learned so far about their new home. When he finally paused, the male on the other side of the window pointed at the device on his arm and then gestured for him to continue. Desmond turned to Infinity. "Your turn."

The device on the creature's wrist spoke again. "Yes, you talk. Talk more."

"That's extraordinary!" said Dr. Fornas. "Would you mind if I take my turn next?"

"Please," Infinity said. "I'm not much of a talker anyway."

Fornas began summarizing the last few years of his life, focusing on how everything had changed after a county sheriff found twenty strangers wandering naked in a national forest in Southern Missouri. Those strangers, including Armando Doyle, claimed to have traveled to this world from an alternate version of Earth—an alternate timeline. The strangers were very convincing, and the entire nation became enthralled by them when Armando provided precise coordinates for locating a radio signal being transmitted by an alien civiliza-tion—a signal that turned out to actually exist. Dr. Fornas explained how he had volunteered to head up a team to look into the implications of the radio signal and the strangers' intriguing stories. The team eventually began to cautiously analyze the Outlanders' instructions for making a bridging device. They then embarked on a massive endeavor to decode the supposed 'key' to unlocking the true potential of bridging technology, a key that consisted of nine hundred symbols tattooed on Armando's back.

When Fornas mentioned the tattoos, Armando turned around and lifted his shirt, revealing about half of the nine hundred symbols. This apparently generated considerable excitement among the strangers, who spoke rapidly to each other for a few seconds.

When Fornas had finished his story, the being in the bridging chamber again gestured for more, so Armando took a turn, adding to the story Desmond and Dr. Fornas had started. He started with how he had become the CEO of the first bridging center on his own version of Earth. This endeavor had gone smoothly until it was discovered that the bridging devices—by this time there were seven worldwide—had been creating a previously undiscovered heavy particle. Millions of these particles had been drifting through the Earth's mantle and collecting at the planet's core. They steadily eroded the core until the damage was irreversible, ultimately causing the planet's collapse, killing over eight billion people.

Armando continued, explaining how a desperate attempt had been made to save a small portion of the human species by bridging colonies to alternate worlds. This effort had continued until the last possible moments. When it was time to bridge out the final colony, the bridging device failed in the process of bridging out the first group of twenty, sending the group to an unknown destination, presumably lost forever. Desmond and Infinity happened to be in this group. Armando and his techs managed to get the bridging device back in working order long enough to bridge out one more group—the twenty people who had appeared on this very world and were found wandering naked in the national forest.

Armando paused and said, "Okay, who's next?"

The voice of the creature's device came over the comm system. "Okay. Yes. We have words you speak."

Desmond turned to the three strangers. The male in the center raised his arm device to his mouth and whispered softly to it while he pressed on it with his other hand. The device translated. "We go out this room now. Speak to you. You open room."

The humans in the viewing room exchanged nervous glances.

Fornas stepped closer to the window. "We don't mean to be rude or inhospitable, but we prefer to speak to you this way. We prefer that you stay inside the bridging chamber for now. I hope you understand."

The male's translator emitted a rapid-fire stream of foreign language. He listened until the device was finished and then whispered into it again. "Easy to talk outside room. Not easy to talk inside room. You open room."

Fornas glanced at Armando and shook his head slightly, apparently at a loss regarding what to do next.

Desmond heard a frustrated growl coming from Infinity's throat. She started to say something, but he held up a finger and whispered to her, "We're guests here, remember? Maybe we should let them handle this." He nodded toward Armando and Fornas.

Infinity narrowed her eyes at him but stayed quiet.

Armando addressed the strangers. "Please forgive us, but we are concerned about the possible spreading of disease. It is clear to us that you are from a version of this world that diverged from ours long ago. Therefore, it's quite possible you could infect us, or we could infect you. Our precautions are for your safety as well as ours. But we certainly want you to feel welcome here, and we do wish to speak with you. We are curious as to who you are and how you got here."

The creature eyed Armando for a moment, apparently waiting to see whether he was going to say more, and then pressed on his translator. The device spewed out another rapid stream of language.

The three strangers glanced at each other. Desmond couldn't be sure, but he thought they might be frowning. The one who had been translating, apparently their spokesperson, whispered into his device again and waited for it to translate. "Outside this structure. We put something there. You go. You see."

Again, the humans exchanged glances.

"We're still in quarantine," Fornas muttered. He stepped

to a control panel on the wall, pressed three different buttons, and said, "Fuller, are you at your desk?"

After a delay of several seconds, a voice came over the comm system. "Sorry, Dr. Fornas. Yes, I'm at my desk now." The guy sounded like he had just sprinted several hundred yards.

"Fuller, I need a favor. Can you take a look around outside the facility and let me know if you see anything out of the ordinary?"

"I don't need to," said Fuller. "I've already seen it. Do you know something about it, Dr. Fornas? It's got everyone on edge out here."

"*What's* got everyone on edge?"

"The structure, or sculpture—whatever it is. I was hoping you could shed some light on what it is and how it got here."

Fornas looked at the strangers beyond the window. "Describe it to me, Fuller. What the hell are we talking about?"

"It's on the front lawn. I don't know how somebody hauled it there without anyone noticing. No one came inside with delivery papers for me to sign, and nobody else saw anything."

"Describe it, Fuller!"

"Sorry. The thing's at least thirty feet tall, shaped like a cone, with a base maybe twenty feet wide. It's painted solid green, like army green or something."

Desmond's eyes met Infinity's. "Oh shit," he heard himself say. He turned to the fur-covered beings in the bridging chamber.

The male in the middle spoke into his translator, which then spoke to the humans. "You open room now. We speak to you."

5

CONSEQUENCES

APRIL 10 - 4:36 PM

"Do what they ask," Infinity said. "Open the bridging chamber."

Fornas shook his head. "That would be terribly reckless. I cannot allow it. They could be carriers of all manner of—"

Infinity grabbed his shoulder. "Listen, goddammit! That green cone outside is exactly like the one we saw this morning before bridging here. These guys have something to do with the destruction of the version of Earth my colony just evacuated. Maybe they caused it, maybe they were trying to prevent it—I don't know. Either way, we have no choice but to cooperate with them."

Fornas rubbed his temples. "My God. I'm completely out of my depth here. I'll have to consult with people who have more authority, perhaps Colonel Chislett. This is a matter of national security."

A voice came over the comm. "Listen to me, goddammit!"

Everyone turned toward the strangers. The words had come from the center male's translator.

The creature whispered into the device, and it translated. "Yes, we have something to do with the destruction of the version of Earth you just evacuated."

Even though the translator had mimicked Infinity's words almost exactly, the slightly different phrasing made it clear that he understood the conversation and was conveying his own coherent response.

He spoke into his translator again. "You open this room. We go out. We talk to you. Now, goddammit."

Infinity turned back to Fornas and raised her brows. "We can't afford to play games with these people. Let them out."

Desmond spoke up. "I think right now we need to be more concerned about destruction of the entire planet than contracting a disease."

Fornas took a deep breath and pushed three buttons on the comm system again. "Fuller?"

"Still here, Dr. Fornas," Fuller said over the comm. "Is everything okay?"

"I need you to get ahold of Colonel Chislett. If he's not available, ask for the next highest ranking authority who is involved with the National Bridging Center. Tell them it's urgent!" Fornas pushed another button and turned to one of the bio-suited techs. "Harwood, alert the Marine squad over in the quarantine bunk room and tell them to take up position outside the bridging chamber hatch. They should come armed."

Harwood turned without a word and left the tiny room.

Infinity turned to the viewing window. The strangers were still standing motionless, waiting. "We want to talk to you," she said. "We're getting ready to open the bridging chamber now." She pointed through the window at the hatch behind the strangers. "We'll be outside that door waiting for you."

The male's device rattled off a translation, and the strangers turned and glanced at the hatch.

Fornas walked out of the viewing room, and the others followed him out the door and through the med lab. "This had better not be a mistake," he said as they all gathered quietly by the bridging chamber hatch.

Seconds later they were joined by eight Marines in paper clothing, each carrying a handheld weapon made of living tissue. As the Marines were assembling into a tactical formation, five more approached, each accompanied by a robotic creature the size and shape of a large dog but which appeared to be constructed of exposed muscles and tendons connected to a white plastic skeletal frame. Infinity had first seen these creatures the previous day, when Armando and the Marines had appeared unexpectedly on the arthropod world. Armando had said the creatures were specialized, bridgeable weapons. They certainly had a wicked, intimidating presence.

Fornas addressed the Marines. "Less than an hour ago, the bridging chamber was somehow breached from another timeline. We have no idea how—"

Infinity interrupted him. "We really can't afford to make these visitors wait any longer." She turned and addressed the Marines. "Three people are going to come through that hatch. They'll look strange to you, maybe even alarming. But it's critical that you do *not* threaten or intimidate them. Don't do anything unless they physically attack. Got it?"

A few of the men nodded. All of them were frowning.

She nodded to Fornas. "Let's do this."

Fornas sighed and, to Infinity's surprise, stepped up to the hatch and opened it himself.

Several of the Marines mumbled curses as the three strangers stepped out.

Infinity immediately noticed a pleasant aroma. Either these beings were fond of perfume, or they naturally smelled like flowers. This smell seemed strangely fitting, considering the stylish, intricate ornamental patterns dyed into their fur.

The strangers stood in the hatch's opening, surveying the med lab and the people facing them. The female pointed to one of the robotic dogs and then muttered something into her translator. "Those devices are for hurt," the translator said. "You take those hurt devices away. We talk when no hurt devices."

"Yes," Fornas said, "those are hurt devices. We call them weapons. We have them here because we don't know whether you want to hurt us. We need to be able to defend ourselves if you try to hurt us."

Again the woman spoke into her device. "You take weapons away now, goddammit. We talk after weapons are away."

Infinity took a few steps toward the strangers and examined them more carefully. Other than the rope-like garments around their waists, which were too skimpy to conceal weapons, they only had the translators attached to their left arms. She turned back to Fornas and Armando. "Unless those translators can also be used as weapons, they appear to be unarmed. I think we should put the weapons away and see what they have to say."

One of the Marines spoke up. "I'm Sergeant Virgil Harrington. I lead this squad of Marines. All of these men have volunteered to put their lives on the line for this bridging program. I don't know who the hell you are, but I know you're not even from this world. I can't imagine what would make you think you get to be in charge."

Infinity leveled her gaze at the Marine and then glanced at the furry strangers, who were watching this conversation intently while the devices on their arms translated what was being said. She turned back to Sergeant Harrington and said, "My name's Infinity, and I have no interest in being in charge. But you need to know we're on the same side. You guys saw what was happening on the world you rescued us from today. You saw that green cone beside the bridge-in site. Well, these creatures have somehow placed one of those cones just outside of this facility. We need to cooperate with them if we don't want the same thing to happen here."

Sergeant Harrington frowned and turned to Fornas. "Is this true?"

Fornas nodded. "We have no idea how it got there, but it's there."

"Jesus!" said the sergeant.

"We have a delicate situation here," Infinity said. "We don't yet know what these beings are capable of."

Harrington pursed his lips and then nodded. He turned to his men. "Shepherd, Epsom, Lowman. Collect the weapons and take them back to the bunk room."

The Marines nodded and started gathering the handheld weapons. Then they took the leashes of the five robot dogs and headed back to their quarters.

Infinity turned back to the three strangers, who were still watching with apparent fascination.

The one who had done most of the talking inside the bridging chamber held his device close to his mouth and whispered into it. When he was done, the translator said, "Now we speak. We are here because you have done things you must not do."

The room grew silent.

"What do you mean?" Armando asked.

The creature replied through his translator. "You have a bridging device."

Armando nodded. "Yes, we do. As we explained, we discovered the instructions for building this device in a radio signal transmitted by an alien civilization we call the Outlanders."

"Yes, the Outlanders," said the being. "The Outlanders sent instructions. We received Outlanders' instructions. We made bridging devices."

Fornas spoke up. "So, what have we done that we weren't supposed to do?"

The three strangers turned their attention to the door on the far side of the room, where Shepherd, Epsom, and Lowman were returning without the weapons. The three Marines took their positions among the others.

The female creature stepped away from the two males and walked toward Infinity. She stopped when she was about two feet away, wafting her distinctly floral scent, which was even more pleasant at close proximity. She stared into Infinity's eyes, and for the first time Infinity noticed her irises were not blue, green, nor brown, but rather a striking golden bronze. The woman studied Infinity's face, apparently fascinated. She lifted a hand and gently touched Infinity's scalp.

"How did you bridge without losing your hair?" Infinity asked.

The woman touched her translator, and it spoke rapidly to her. She whispered her reply, and the translator said, "It is important that you ask how. What you ask tells us information about you."

That wasn't even close to an answer. What information had Infinity just given them? She was tempted to ask again but decided to hold off.

The woman lifted Infinity's paper shirt and peered underneath, and Infinity had to fight the urge to slap away her hand. The woman returned the shirt to its original position and looked into Infinity's eyes again.

"Infinity," the woman said, without the use of her translator, obviously trying to slow the word down to match the pace of human speech.

"Yes, I'm Infinity. What is your name?"

The woman's translator spewed out at least a dozen words in less than two seconds. She smiled and spoke to her device, which then said, "You cannot speak my name. You make name for me."

Infinity fought back a smile. "Okay, I'll call you Kitty."

Again the woman slowed down her speech. "Kitt-ee."

Infinity nodded to the man behind her who had first spoken to the humans. "We'll call him Tigger." She shifted her gaze to the other man. "And we'll call him, um... Teddy. Is that okay with you?"

The woman listened to her translator and then replied. "Yes. Okay with us."

Fornas interjected, "What have we done that we were not supposed to do?"

Kitty spoke through her translator. "We have procedures. You must do our procedures. Procedures are for to help the Outlanders. Outlanders are important and wise and foremost. You did not do our procedures."

Armando cleared his throat, "Are you saying there are rules that are supposed to be followed that we broke?"

"Yes, you did not follow procedures. You broke rule." The woman pointed to Armando's chest and gave a curt spin of her finger, apparently telling him to turn around to show his tattoos of the nine hundred symbols again.

Armando turned and lifted his shirt far enough to expose

about a third of the symbols. "What rule are we breaking?" he asked.

"You have key to bridging technology," she said. "It is there, on your back."

Armando lowered his shirt and turned back around. "Yes. This key was given to us." He nodded toward Desmond. "To him, actually. He was on a version of this world that was occupied by beings he called mongrels. The mongrels were kind enough to give him the key to bridging technology."

The woman turned and rapidly exchanged a few phrases with Tigger and Teddy.

Tigger stepped forward and whispered into his translator. "The mongrels broke rule. Rule is do not give key to bridging technology. When you give key to bridging technology, we must give consequences. We gave consequences to mongrels. They will not give key to bridging technology again."

Infinity felt her chest begin tightening. "What do you mean, you gave consequences? What did you do to them?"

"Mongrels bridge to many worlds. We destroy all worlds mongrels bridge to."

Infinity stared, trying to comprehend the implications of what the creature had just said.

Desmond cleared his throat. "You destroyed every one of the worlds the mongrels have bridged to?"

"Yes, we gave consequences."

Desmond ran his hand over his scalp. "The world we were on when the mongrels gave me the key to bridging technology —did you destroy that world?"

"Yes. We destroy all worlds mongrels bridge to."

"Hundreds of our people were on that world," Infinity said. "And there were probably millions of others living there. Those people didn't deserve to be killed!"

"We gave consequences. Mongrels will not give key to

bridging technology again. Now mongrels must convince us that we should not destroy mongrel home world."

Infinity suddenly felt the urge to kick this fuzzy asshole in the face, to break his jaw and then keep kicking until his head was nothing more than a pile of goo on the floor.

"Did you destroy the world we were on earlier today?" Desmond asked. "Is that why that green cone was there?"

"Yes. That green cone make heavy particles. You know about heavy particles. Bridging device with no key make small number heavy particles. That green cone make large number heavy particles. Bridging device with no key destroy world slowly. Green cone destroy world quickly. We gave consequences. Mongrels gave key to bridging technology to you. Consequences for mongrels. Consequences for you. That green cone."

A grave silence permeated the med lab. Infinity glanced around at the faces of the other humans. They were all frowning, but she wasn't sure they understood fully what was happening.

"So you're just going to destroy this world and the billions of people who live here?" Desmond asked.

After the man's device had translated these words, the three strangers lowered their translators and exchanged a few phrases in their own language. The woman then spoke to her device again. "The mongrels gave the key to bridging technology to you. We gave consequences to mongrels. We do not know how many others you gave key to bridging technology to. Because we do not know, we destroy all worlds you bridge to. Rule is do not give key to bridging technology."

"We haven't given the key to anyone else!" Infinity said, trying unsuccessfully to keep her anger under control.

The woman pointed to the Marines and spoke into her

translator. "You gave key to bridging technology to people of this world."

Dr. Fornas turned abruptly to Sergeant Harrington. "You need to bring those weapons back out. These people are clearly a threat!"

"Wait!" Infinity said. "If you don't see that they're capable of destroying this planet whether you're armed or not, then you really haven't been paying attention."

Harrington shifted his gaze from Fornas to Infinity, and then to the three strangers. "She's right. We should hold off on the weapons. At least for the moment."

Fornas muttered a curse. Infinity ignored him as she turned back to the strangers. "Okay, you have our attention. You said you wanted to talk to us, so I assume you haven't started destroying this world. Let's talk."

The woman listened to the translation and then replied. "The Outlanders are important and wise and foremost. They had purpose for radio signal with instructions for bridging device. The purpose is destroy worlds with beings that do not understand key to bridging technology. Beings that understand should live. Beings that do not understand should not live. This purpose is important and wise and foremost. We help Outlanders. We give consequences to beings that break rule."

Armando said, "So you've taken it upon yourselves to enforce the Outlanders' rules? Have you ever even met the Outlanders? Their radio signal travelled tens of thousands of light years to get to this world—their civilization probably doesn't even exist anymore."

The strangers listened to the translation and then frowned. The woman spoke again. "The Outlanders are important and wise and foremost."

It was starting to sound like these people actually

worshipped the Outlanders, a thought that didn't comfort Infinity in the least. She closed her eyes for a moment, trying to absorb the shock of learning that these people had not only destroyed the world that had been her home for the last nineteen months, but they may also have destroyed the other human colonies she had worked to save. If these bastards were telling the truth about having destroyed all the worlds the humans of Infinity's Earth had bridged to, then the only survivors of her home world were the thirty-six refugees who were now living on this world. She took a deep breath and tried to suppress her anger, but she could feel her control slipping away. She opened her eyes and looked directly at the woman. "We don't want you to destroy this world. We would like to convince you not to do that. But I want you to know that if you *do* try to do that, I will kill you before you can even think about bridging back to your world. I will kill you with my bare hands."

"So much for trying not to intimidate them," Sergeant Harrington said from behind Infinity. "Marines, move in closer. Be ready to take them out by any means necessary."

The men moved forward until they were no more than two feet from the strangers and formed a circle around them.

The strangers were still frowning, but they didn't look at all intimidated.

The woman spoke into her translator. "You did not understand the key to bridging technology. You destroy your home world with bridging device. Mongrels give the key to bridging technology to you. You use the key to build this bridging device." She gestured to the hatch behind her. "You break the rule. We give you consequences. We destroy all worlds you bridge to. Your home world destroyed, and all worlds you bridge to destroyed. Now this world is your home world. So, like mongrels, you must show us that we should not destroy your home world."

Infinity felt her hands turning into fists. Kitty noticed this, glancing down briefly, but she showed no signs of fear or anger. Either these beings were confident in their ability to fend off attacks, or they were able to bridge out within a split second.

Fornas said, "What do we have to do to show you that you should not destroy this world?"

The woman listened as her device translated, and then she spoke. "Like the mongrels, you must show us by bridging to a world we choose for you. We will watch what you do on that world. What you do on that world will show us that we should destroy your home world. Or what you do on that world will show us that we should not destroy your home world. This is how we decide. We decide this way many times before. The key to bridging technology was given to you. You did not understand the key until it was given to you. Now you show us that you deserve to have the key to bridging technology."

Infinity's fists were now balled so tightly that they hurt. She took a breath and focused on relaxing them. "You're giving us a test? You're making us take a goddamn test to prove that we're worthy of staying alive?"

The woman listened and then replied, "Yes."

Infinity took a step closer. "I have a better idea. How about if we kill you right now and bridge your mangled bodies to a world where they'll be eaten by rats?"

Several of the Marines pressed forward until their faces were inches from the strangers. Apparently the soldiers were as eager to rip these fuzzy bastards apart as Infinity was.

"Please," Fornas said, "let's not anger them unnecessarily."

Kitty smiled at Infinity and said, "We want you to observe."

Abruptly, she and the two creatures were gone. Three faint pops echoed through the room as air rushed in to fill the empty space where their bodies had been.

"Shit!" Infinity grumbled.

"What does this mean?" Sergeant Harrington asked. "What do they want us to observe?"

No one seemed to have an answer to this, and the group fell into uneasy silence, waiting for something to happen.

After about two minutes, Kitty stuck her head out of the open bridging chamber and stepped through the hatch, followed by Tigger and Teddy. Kitty spoke into her translator. "We give consequences many times. You do not surprise us when you are angry and try to hurt us. Outside this structure. You go and see." She then waited silently, with the two men on either side of her.

Fornas stepped over to the wall and pushed a few buttons on a control panel similar to the one in the viewing room. "Fuller? You there?"

"I'm here, Dr. Fornas. Folks out here are pretty frightened. We'd like to know what's going on. Seth Stanway just told me there are now two of the green cones outside. Apparently one of them is doing something. He said it's making a noise of some kind. Should we be concerned?"

"Just tell everyone to stay calm," Fornas said. He pushed a button and turned back to the three strangers. "Have you activated one of those cones? You said you'd give us a chance to prove ourselves!"

Kitty listened to the translation and then replied. "Those cones are ready to give you consequences. You observe we can bring more cones. Only one cone is needed for destroy your world. But now you see. If you destroy cone, we bring more cones. We give you consequences. We destroy your world, unless you show us that we should not destroy your world."

Infinity scanned the faces of the humans in the room. Most of them, including Desmond, looked as if they had no idea what to do next. She sighed and turned to Kitty. "Alright, what do we have to do?"

6

BRIDGE-OUT

APRIL 10 - 6:11 PM

ALL FOURTEEN OF Desmond's fellow colonists sat before him, crammed into one of the quarantine living quarters, waiting to hear what he and Infinity had to say. These people were his family, the only real family he'd had since leaving his mom's house for college. All of them were tough and resourceful—they had proven it during the last nineteen months. But everyone except Gideon now had partners and families. Desmond couldn't ask them to join a team bridging to an unknown destination. To complete a mysterious test for which the result of failing was the destruction of a world with billions of people on it. If the team failed the test, everyone here would likely die, but at least they would have had a few relatively peaceful hours or days first.

"That's all we know at this time," he said, having just finished describing the events that had taken place in the med lab during the last hour.

Infinity, who had been pacing back and forth with frustration, stopped and said, "At first the bastards were only going to let one human participate in this insane test. But we insisted on sending a group, and they didn't seem to care much one way or the other. They're making us do it now—like within the next half hour. They won't let us wait for more specialized people to get here. Sergeant Harrington has volunteered his squad of Marines for the team." She nodded toward Desmond. "We almost had to fight them to get them to let any of us on the team. I think the only reason they allowed it is that we've had more extensive bridging experience."

"I'd like to be on the team," Gideon said flatly.

Desmond nodded. "We figured you would, and we already got it approved. The rest of you, though, well, we didn't think...."

"We understand, Desmond," said Hayley Millwright. "You don't have to explain."

"Emily and I would go if you needed us," said Steven, "but we trust you guys to do what needs to be done." Other than Gideon, Steven and Emily were the last surviving National Guardsmen in the group.

"We appreciate the gesture," Infinity said, "but it's a moot point, anyway. The Marines don't want any more than three of us."

Lenny, sitting on the bed with Daisy on his lap, said, "So that's all those hairballs told you? You don't have any idea what you're supposed to accomplish in order to save our sorry asses?"

Desmond sighed and shook his head. "They wouldn't tell us. No idea what kind of world we're bridging to, no idea what we're supposed to do when we get there. But apparently they're going to be watching everything we do."

Infinity said, "They might want to test our resilience, or maybe observe how compassionate we are. Or maybe test our problem-solving skills. There's just no way to know."

"So let me get this straight," Xavier said. "You're going to bridge there now, meaning it'll be almost sunset, and you'll have no idea what you're supposed to do."

Desmond nodded. "That about sums it up."

Gideon stepped forward, a grim expression on his face. "No sense putting it off."

The others came forward and took turns hugging Desmond, Infinity, and Gideon. After everyone had said goodbye, the three left the room and walked back to the med lab.

In the lab, the Marines were milling around the bridging chamber hatch, outfitted in their organic fatigues again. The Marine named Shepherd noticed Desmond, Infinity, and Gideon and handed each of them a transparent bag containing a set of fatigues. "We got a few extras," he said. "Thought you might like the chance to bridge with something on besides your birthday suits. Don't worry about the fit—they're all one size. They adjust themselves to fit your body. It's a little creepy the first time it happens."

Desmond reached into his bag and felt the black material. It was like touching a dead snake. "This really is living tissue?"

Shepherd shrugged. "That's what they tell me. I don't know much about it. I know it actually has living cells. But there ain't no nerves or brain or nothing like that. Beats being naked."

Desmond's eyes met Infinity's. He half-expected her to turn down the offer and do without, but instead she nodded and thanked the Marine.

Shepherd pointed at a pair of doors. "You can put them on in those exam rooms if you want."

Gideon went into one of the rooms, and Desmond and Infinity took the other. Desmond pulled one of the items from his bag. It was a helmet, identical to the ones the Marines had been wearing when he'd first seen them the previous evening. He set it aside and pulled out the next item, a shirt, which was big and rather heavy. It had thick, armor-like sections covering the chest and abdomen, but otherwise it looked like a simple pullover.

Desmond removed his paper shirt and pulled on the black garment. It felt like slightly-moist leather against his skin. No wonder the Marines had been anxious to get out of their fatigues.

"It's too freaking big," Infinity said. She had also pulled hers on, and it was hanging loosely from her shoulders.

Desmond started to make a comment about how fashionable she looked, but then he stopped and stared. "Holy crap, your shirt's moving."

She nodded at him. "So is yours."

Desmond could feel it now. The garment was contracting, pulling in on itself. He knew that it was just adjusting its fit, but Shepherd had been right—the feeling was creepy. Desmond had to fight the urge to yank the shirt off.

Infinity groaned in displeasure as she stared down at her garment. "This doesn't comfort me in the least."

The next items they pulled from the bags were pants, which were heavy and oversized like the shirts. They put them on, waited for them to shrink, and then they pulled out the shoes, which looked like black leather slippers. The soles appeared to be thickened in the same way the chest armor was. They both slipped their feet into the shoes, which began shrinking seconds later. Once they were both fully dressed, they stood dubiously admiring each other's perfectly-fitting fatigues.

Infinity pointed at the helmet she'd placed on the exam table. "I don't know about you, but I'm not putting that thing on my head."

Desmond agreed, so they left the helmets and rejoined the others in the lab. Gideon emerged at the same time, having apparently also decided against the helmet.

Shepherd was waiting for them with three handheld organic weapons. The devices were about eighteen inches long. Each had a handle and trigger guard, but otherwise they looked more like something cut from an animal's leg than a gun.

"We decided not to take the dogs," Shepherd said, "but these things are just as handy. They fire dense, dart-like projectiles at surprising muzzle velocity. Six hundred feet per second, believe it or not. They manage that with nothing more than muscle contraction and elastic tendons. They're downright deadly. I'll give you a rundown on how to operate them."

Desmond knew without a doubt that Infinity wouldn't want to use these weapons, and he knew that she wouldn't bother to use a diplomatic tone in refusing them, so he decided to speak up first. "I prefer to bridge without a weapon."

Shepherd raised his brows. "We have no idea what we'll encounter."

"Which is why I don't want one either," Infinity said. "I've learned to be cautious because I've never been able to bridge with a weapon. Feeling vulnerable is what keeps me alive."

Shepherd seemed a little surprised by this, but he nodded and then turned to Gideon. "And you?"

Gideon hesitated, glancing at Desmond and Infinity.

Then he reached for one of the weapons. "Show me how it works."

Shepherd handed it to him. "There ain't much to it." He pointed to a bulge in front of the trigger guard. "The magazine contains twelve projectiles. There ain't a projectile in the chamber right now because—as crazy as it sounds—when the projectiles are pushed up out of the magazine and into the chamber, they get cut free from the body of the weapon and die pretty quickly. This allows them to be fired, but they won't bridge once they've been severed from the main body. So don't rack one into the chamber until we get there."

The Marine pointed to a lever on the magazine that appeared to be made of white bone. "When you're ready, just pull that back firmly to chamber the first projectile." He moved his finger to a smaller lever near the trigger guard. "That's the safety. Push it forward before firing. Pull it back when you're done." He moved his finger again. "And that's the trigger. After you fire the first projectile, the second one will automatically move up into the chamber. Chambering takes a full two seconds. I know—slow as shit. It helps to count out the two seconds. After you've fired all twelve projectiles, the weapon becomes useless. They're disposable and can't be reloaded." He shook his head and chuckled. "Some of the guys say these weapons are actually *grown* in big test tubes, but I don't believe it."

Gideon hefted the weapon and nodded. "Let's hope we don't have to use them."

The four of them moved over and joined the rest of the Marines, who were waiting silently near the bridging chamber hatch.

Sergeant Harrington, Fornas, and Armando entered the lab through a door on the far side of the room. "Okay, listen up!" Harrington said. "We just finished conferring with

Colonel Chislett. The colonel doesn't believe we are the right people for this mission, and he made no secret of the fact that those above him don't either. He wants to take the time to put together a team of specialists, including scholars, politicians, and God knows who else. Problem is, we don't have that kind of time. Based on what Dr. Fornas and I have seen, we agree that this threat is real, and that we need to take any actions necessary to neutralize it. I told Colonel Chislett to assemble his team and get them here ASAP. But I also made it clear to him that if we can't convince these fuzzy fuckers to give us more time, we're going to comply with their request and complete the test ourselves."

Desmond heard a rapid string of foreign language coming from a translator behind him. He turned to see Kitty standing in the bridging chamber's open hatch. She whispered into her device, which then said, "Yes, you comply with our request now. You do not wait. We have reasons for no waiting. You come now." She gestured for them to enter the chamber.

Everyone turned to Harrington.

The sergeant nodded grimly. "God help us." He then stepped forward and followed Kitty into the chamber.

Tigger and Teddy were waiting inside. Next to them was a vehicle. Or a machine. The thing was basically pill-shaped, with a diameter of about four feet. Numerous appendages of various sizes and lengths were folded up, resting neatly against the object's main body. Several transparent windows revealed a cockpit inside with a single seat surrounded by rows of what appeared to be controls.

Kitty pointed to a pile of smaller objects on the floor that looked identical to the translating devices worn by the strangers. Kitty whispered into her device, "We allow you to use translators. You may choose to use them, or you may choose to not use them."

Tigger stepped forward and held out a fistful of what appeared to be thin, three-inch-long wires. He spoke through his translator. "We will put these in you. These devices allow Kitty to observe what you do. You will show us that we should give you consequences. Or you will show us that we should not give you consequences."

"What the hell are those things?" Infinity asked.

Tigger plucked one of the wires from his hand and held it up. "Device for Kitty to observe. I will put device in your head. Kitty will bridge with you and will be inside that machine." He gestured toward the spherical vehicle. "Kitty will observe what you do. Device in your head will allow Kitty to see what you see, hear what you hear, watch what you do."

"Like a camera and microphone?" Harrington asked.

"Camera and microphone," Tigger replied through his translator.

Desmond decided to try one more time to get some guidance. "We would still like to know what we are supposed to do to convince you not to destroy this world. We understand that you have rules, but we can't follow those rules if we don't know what they are."

Tigger's device translated, and he whispered back into it. "We cannot observe what you do if we tell you what to do. We must observe what you choose to do." He handed most of the wires to Teddy but kept one. He then stepped forward and placed one hand firmly on Desmond's scalp. With his other hand he held the three-inch wire near Desmond's forehead as if preparing to push the end of it directly into his skin.

Desmond considered pulling back and refusing, but what good would that do? Instead, he gritted his teeth and waited, concentrating on the man's strangely pleasant smell to distract himself.

Tigger pushed the wire in, puncturing the skin above

Desmond's right eye. He then angled the wire toward Desmond's temple and threaded it in farther. Desmond winced as he felt the wire working its way under his skin around the side of his skull. Tigger then pressed on the protruding end with his thumb, forcing it in until it was flush with the skin's surface. He wiped at it once, stepped back, and spoke rapidly for a few seconds without bothering to translate for the humans' benefit.

Kitty quickly replied, also without translating, and Desmond realized she had opened a hatch on the side of the capsule and was now sitting in the cockpit. Tigger gave Desmond a quick smile, plucked another of the wires from Teddy's palm, and moved next to Gideon.

Desmond touched his forehead gingerly. It was a bit sore, and he could feel a slight bump where the camera was, but his fingers came away with no blood. With nothing else to do but wait for Tigger to finish inserting the rest of the cameras, Desmond gathered up a few of the translators and started handing them out. One of the Marines grabbed the rest and began helping.

Once the translators had been distributed, Desmond inspected his more closely. It looked like a lumpy wrist brace, with one large hole for his fingers and a smaller hole for his thumb. He slipped his left hand into it and was surprised to find that it was comfortable and snug.

He stepped over to Teddy and held up the device. "How do we use these?" The translator almost immediately emitted a rapid sequence of foreign words.

Teddy replied, and Desmond's translator said, "You are using it now."

Desmond gazed down at the device. He then realized his translator and the others given to the humans were slightly smaller than those worn by the three strangers. "I guess we get the basic model, translator for dummies," he muttered. The device didn't translate this, perhaps because it didn't hear him, or perhaps because it was smart enough to know he wasn't really talking to anyone in particular. The second possibility seemed more likely, although it made Desmond feel uneasy.

When Tigger had finished inserting the last body camera, Kitty pulled the capsule hatch closed, sealing herself inside.

Tigger and Teddy moved closer together until they were shoulder to shoulder. "You bridge now," Tigger said through his translator. "We observe what you do." Without another word, the two strangers vanished.

Desmond wondered how they were able to bridge out at will like that. Apparently they had transcended the restrictions on bridging technology he was used to, including the need to administer a radioisotope marker.

Kitty remained seated in the capsule, gazing out calmly at the confused humans.

Sergeant Harrington turned to Fornas and Armando. "Unless you're coming with us, you might want to exit the chamber."

"Yes, of course," Fornas said, scurrying toward the door. "Good luck to you all."

Armando hesitated. "It's only half an hour until sunset," he said, addressing the entire group but making a point of leveling his gaze at Desmond and Infinity. "You should probably find a sheltered place to rest until morning." He paused. "It's unfortunate that we don't know what behaviors these beings are hoping to observe, but if you follow your own hearts, I'm sure you will adequately impress them. You are the best that humanity has to offer. I'm proud to be represented by you." With that, he turned and exited the bridging chamber.

Suddenly the sound of knocking resonated through the

bridging chamber. Desmond and the others turned to see Kitty rapping her knuckles on the inside of one of the capsule's windows. She flicked her wrist rapidly, waving for them to come closer. They all gathered around the pod.

Kitty inspected the group around her, apparently making sure they were near enough, and then she turned her attention to the controls.

Desmond felt a wet prickling on his skin, and then the bridging chamber disappeared.

DESMOND TEETERED FOR A MOMENT, experiencing only a brief moment of nausea. Still on his feet, he scanned his surroundings. The first thing that hit him was the smell—like a mixture of rotting garbage and animal feces. He threw a hand over his nose and mouth and looked toward the west. The sun was a faint, orange ball hanging above the horizon, nearly obscured by a haze that permeated the sky. To the north, several miles away, he saw dozens of glistening buildings, some of them as tall as skyscrapers. Much closer, scrubby, pale-green plants were growing haphazardly between crudely-constructed shacks and piles of trash. People were emerging from some of the shacks and approaching Desmond and the others. Looking closer, he realized they weren't people at all. The creatures were walking on two legs, but their heads were too large to be human, and their torsos were wide and squat, making their arms and legs look strikingly long by comparison. Even stranger, each of them had a bushy tail at least three feet long that bobbed up and down as they walked.

"Do not do anything threatening!" Sergeant Harrington ordered. "We're here to prove we deserve to exist, and I'm pretty damn sure starting trouble with the locals won't earn us any points."

Desmond turned to Infinity. She frowned and shook her head. He knew exactly what she was thinking—that if they wanted to avoid trouble, they shouldn't have come armed to the teeth. Infinity wouldn't hesitate to finish a fight that had already started, but she preferred to avoid conflict altogether.

At least twenty of the creatures were cautiously approaching now, and Desmond could see numerous others in the distance staring toward the bridge-in site. Every creature in sight was dressed in a pale-tan, tightly-fitting bodysuit—even the children. As the onlookers drew nearer, Desmond was able to see their facial features in more detail. Two enormous eyes, almost perfectly round and easily two inches in diameter, dominated each creature's face. A small, pointed snout was positioned below the eyes, and below that was an expressive, flexible mouth. Their ears, perhaps twice the size of human ears, protruded near the top of the head on each side, and were so thin that the setting sun shown through them from behind. Their faces reminded Desmond vaguely of some of the primitive primates that had lived on his own version of Earth, such as tarsiers and lemurs.

As the creatures drew nearer, they began speaking to each other, in a language completely unfamiliar to Desmond. The sounds mostly consisted of whistles, growls, and chittering clicks.

A crowd began gathering, and Desmond noticed that some of their bodysuits were filthy and torn in places. He also noticed something else—every one of these creatures was lean and fit. There wasn't an obese or gaunt individual among them, although he did spot a female that was clearly pregnant. She was with a group of four others who were all slightly smaller than most of the adults, perhaps the equivalent of teenagers. This group was particularly vocal, jabbering loudly and pointing at the humans. Perhaps they were asking questions. They seemed to be growing increasingly frustrated that Desmond and his companions weren't responding.

Soon the crowd surrounding the humans had grown to at least thirty. They were understandably curious, but their increasing level of agitation suggested they were suspicious and might soon become threatening.

None of the Marines were making any attempt to communicate, so Desmond raised both his hands in a placating gesture and said, "Hello! I know you can't understand us yet, but we'd like to communicate with you." He pointed to the translator on his arm. "All you have to do is continue talking, and this—"

Suddenly, the creatures before Desmond shifted their attention to something behind him, pointing and chattering excitedly. He turned to look. Kitty's capsule was now standing up, supported by dozens of short, robotic legs. The capsule started making a hissing sound that was subtle at first but quickly increased in volume, and then a small explosion on the capsule's nose expelled a blast of smoke or water vapor.

Cries of surprise or anger erupted from the surrounding crowd. Desmond spun around. The pregnant female was sprawled on the ground, blood spewing from a massive wound in her abdomen. Her companions were staring down at her in shock, and some of the larger adults were beginning to gather around. A few of them kneeled to examine her. But Desmond could tell by the severity of the wound that she was dead.

Desmond heard a mechanical chittering behind him, and he spun around again. The legs beneath Kitty's capsule were now a blur of motion, throwing dirt out in every direction. The capsule was dropping quickly downward into the hole that it was excavating. Seconds later, the entire thing was below the surface, and the tips of numerous robotic arms were scooping dirt from the hole's perimeter and flipping it on top of the capsule. The arms continued working until the hole was filled and nothing remained in its place but a slight mound of disturbed soil. Kitty and the capsule were gone, completely buried.

7

____

NEGOTIATION

APRIL *10* - *7:08 PM*

"WELL, SHIT!" Sergeant Harrington said.

Infinity assessed the creatures gathered around the dead female. None of the beings appeared to be carrying weapons, but something about their muscular build and the way they carried themselves told her they probably weren't harmless pacifists. Which meant that, within seconds, the situation was probably going to escalate into further violence. Kitty had obviously put the humans in this situation on purpose, to watch how they handled the situation. Unfortunately, Infinity had no idea what Kitty considered a good versus a bad response.

"Chamber your projectiles," Harrington ordered, his voice nearly drowned out by the agitated squeaks and barks from the surrounding creatures.

The Marines complied. Gideon glanced at Infinity and then readied his own weapon.

Desmond turned to face Harrington. "We need to give our translators a chance to learn their language. We have to explain to them that we aren't looking for trouble!" Desmond held his wrist device to his mouth and spoke into it, but the translator remained silent.

Infinity could see there wasn't going to be time to wait for the translators. Several of the creatures were already moving toward the humans. Their eyes were still perfectly round, making it difficult to discern any kind of facial expression, but their frantic, guttural cries made it clear they were pissed off.

In an attempt to prevent the Marines from opening fire, Infinity stepped in front of the nearest approaching creature and held up her hands, palms out, signaling it to stop.

The creature didn't even hesitate. It lunged forward and tried to grab Infinity's wrist. She pulled back out of its reach and shouted, "Stop!"

The creature paused and blinked its enormous eyes. The others to its left and right also stopped advancing and stared. Then the nearest creature crouched low, bending at the knees and waist. It positioned its arms in a pronounced pose, touching the ground with the fingertips of its left hand and clenching its right hand into a fist near its cheek, elbow held horizontally to the side. The pose was distinctively nonhuman, but Infinity's gut told her it was a fighting stance. The other creatures took a few steps back and began rattling off loud, agitated barks, clicks, and whistles.

The translator on Infinity's wrist spoke up for the first time. "Kill. Violence. Encouragement." That didn't sound good.

The crouching creature began flicking its bushy tail up and down, the way an angry squirrel would. Infinity instinctively took up a defensive stance, spacing her feet apart and tensing her muscles.

Gideon positioned himself beside her and aiming his weapon at the creature. "Get behind me," he said.

She stepped in front of him instead. "No, you stay behind *me*. Let's see how this plays out before you start shooting."

Most of the creatures had now gathered around the humans, leaving the female Kitty had killed lying in the dirt. Infinity suspected that they were more interested in the possibility of a fight than in the slain woman.

Infinity's translator spoke again, interpreting the mood of the noisy crowd. "Kill. Violence. Encouragement." Perhaps if Infinity fought the creature that was preparing to attack her, she might foster some mutual respect between the two species. This was a big *if*, but it was worth a try.

She sighed and took a step toward the creature. She hated fighting nonhuman animals—they were too unpredictable. She waved her fingers for the creature to come at her, hoping it would understand the gesture. It immediately leapt into the air, reaching a surprising height before coming down at a 45-degree angle, its arms and legs spread wide, exposing its vulnerable torso and groin. Infinity had never seen an attack like this, but the creature's obvious vulnerability tipped her off that the move had to be a feint—a distraction.

Instead of dodging to the side, she threw a hard right and slammed the base of her palm into her attacker's face.

Infinity's brute-force response took the creature by surprise, stopping whatever maneuver it had been planning. She was tempted to take the creature to the ground immediately and immobilize it, but she decided to see how it reacted to her punch first. It landed on its feet and took a step back, managing to stay upright. It blinked its round eyes and gazed at her, but she had no idea how to interpret its nonhuman expression.

"I don't want to hurt you, but I will if you force me to,"

Infinity said. The device on her wrist translated, emitting a series of animal-like sounds.

The creature flicked its eyes toward the device but otherwise didn't respond. She doubted that the translator was working very effectively, having heard so little of the animals' language. A poor translation might make things even worse.

Sergeant Harrington's voice rose above the noise of the crowd. "Infinity, picking a fight isn't exactly a peace-making gesture. What do you think you're doing?"

"I'm negotiating," she said.

Her attacker advanced again before she could elaborate on her answer. This time the creature came in slow, circling to her right, inching closer, flicking its tail rapidly. She watched it carefully, waiting to see what it would try next.

The creature feinted back to the left slightly and then rushed forward, grabbing Infinity around her waist and taking her down before she could move out of the way. She curled her back just before hitting the ground and rolled her attacker over her head. For a moment she was on top of the creature, but it somehow continued the roll's momentum, forcing her all the way over and to the ground again. Before she could get her bearings, the creature was on top of her and had landed two brain-jarring punches to her forehead. Before she knew what was happening, it had locked its long fingers around her throat. Infinity threw her forearms between the thing's wrists and thrust outward, breaking free from its grip. She immediately threw a jab below its chin, connecting with its throat.

The creature choked and coughed, its eyes wide. Its face suddenly disintegrated. Blood, bone, and soft tissue showered onto Infinity, and the creature's body collapsed to the side.

She rolled onto her stomach and jumped to her feet in time to see several of the Marines lowering their weapons. "What the hell?" she cried. "I told you I was negotiating!"

Screams and growls erupted from the crowd of creatures as they realized what had just happened. Several of them moved forward aggressively. This emboldened the others to move closer, and soon the entire crowd was rushing in to attack.

Infinity thrust her palm into the chest of the nearest creature, knocking it to the side. Another moved in and took its place, leaping up with its arms raised, ready to slam its fists down onto her skull. A projectile hit the creature's neck, and it went limp. Infinity tried to dodge the falling body, but it struck her arm as it collapsed into a heap on the ground. Another creature was quickly approaching when a projectile knocked it off its feet and sent gore flying from the back of its head.

The Marines took out another dozen attackers, dropping them in their tracks, forcing those behind them to leap over the bodies in order to advance. Still, more kept going down, killed or maimed by the Marines' nearly silent weapons.

"Fall back!" Sergeant Harrington shouted. "We're moving out, to the east, away from the city!"

Someone grabbed Infinity's elbow, and she turned. It was Desmond, blood flowing down the side of his face from a gash on his scalp.

"We have to go," he said, "or they're going to leave us behind."

Infinity could hardly contain her anger. She glanced at the crowd. At least fifty shouting, growling creatures were lined up, now holding their distance just beyond dozens of bodies scattered in a semicircle. This was a goddamn disaster. Kitty, who had started the conflict in the first place, was no doubt observing the entire spectacle from the safety of her buried capsule.

"Let's move!" Gideon said to Infinity and Desmond. The

guardsman was hanging back, waiting for them as the Marines retreated.

Desmond pulled on her arm.

She shook him off. "Alright, I'm coming!"

The creatures began circling to the southeast to cut them off, but the Marines shot several of them, forcing the attackers to move back again to a safer distance. The furious crowd was growing larger by the second, and the Marines wouldn't be able to hold them much longer.

"Oh, great," Gideon said, staring back toward the bridge-in site. "I think the cavalry just arrived."

Infinity followed his gaze. Several hundred yards away, two animals the size of horses but with shorter legs were approaching. She squinted, struggling to make out details in the fading light. No, they weren't animals—they were mechanical, spider-like robots, each with one of the lemur-like creatures riding on its back. The robots were vehicles. The lemurs controlling them were outfitted in black bodysuits instead of the tan suits worn by all the other creatures.

"Wait, this could be a good thing," Desmond said, pausing to stare at the approaching robots and their riders.

"We just slaughtered thirty of their people," Infinity said. "How could it possibly be good for us that the cops are showing up?"

Desmond shook his head. "I don't know! Maybe they'll get things under control so we can try to explain."

"Move it, you three," Harrington shouted. "Now!" The Marines were still running to the east.

Infinity knew it'd be suicide to get separated from the Marines now. "Come on," she said. She started jogging to catch up, and Desmond and Gideon followed. Looking over her shoulder, she saw that the crowd of lemurs was pursuing them but staying back at a safe distance.

If the robot-riding lemurs really were some kind of police, they would probably stop first to get at least a cursory explanation from the crowd before pursuing the humans. This might be the only opportunity to get away.

Infinity and the others caught up to the Marines, and the group started running at full speed, weaving their way between shacks and piles of rubbish, startling countless lemur creatures who were apparently unaware of the deadly conflict. The ground in the area was hard-packed dirt, and there were no orderly streets. Each shack seemed to be randomly situated with no regard for the positions of the other shacks. It was now almost dark, and lights were glowing within many of the dwellings. With any luck, enough of the locals would have withdrawn to their homes for the night that the humans would be able to avoid another confrontation.

After running about a quarter mile, Infinity glanced back over her shoulder. The angry crowd was no longer in sight. A few lemur creatures were staring from the doorways of their shacks, but it appeared that nobody was pursuing the humans. But then one of the spider vehicles came into view from behind a pile of garbage, followed by the second. The vehicles were moving surprisingly fast, their legs a blur in the twilight. At this rate, it wouldn't take them long to catch up.

"Faster!" Infinity shouted at the Marines ahead of her.

The entire group poured on the speed. One of the Marines tripped and fell, causing two more to pile on top of him. They scrambled to their feet, muttering curses, and resumed running.

After running another hundred yards or so, the vehicles had nearly overtaken them.

"Stop!" Harrington shouted. "Ready your weapons."

The spiders slowed to a stop as the Marines turned on

them and spread into a wide formation, some of them kneeling and those behind them standing.

"Stay behind me," Gideon said to Infinity and Desmond, aiming his weapon at one of the mounted creatures.

Infinity was still worried that slaughtering these beings was the wrong approach. But things had already gone south, and survival was the first priority now.

At such close range, the vehicles looked less like actual spiders and more like motorcycles with six long, segmented legs instead of wheels. Various contraptions protruded from each vehicle's main body, any of which could have been some kind of weapon. The vehicles' operators were similar to all the other lemurs Infinity had seen, aside from having different bodysuits. These suits were black but included several colored bands encircling the ankles just above the creatures' bare feet. One of the lemurs emitted a sequence of chattering, whistling sounds, obviously addressing the humans. Gideon's translator was the only one to respond, perhaps because he was nearest the creatures. "You kill. You have weapons. No weapons."

"We are new here," Harrington said, speaking slowly. "We didn't intend to hurt anyone, and we don't know your rules about weapons." Seconds later, Harrington's wrist device translated this into screeches and barks.

The creature listened and then replied. Gideon's device translated. "No weapons. You give to us weapons."

"We can't do that," Harrington said. "We need to be able to defend ourselves in case you intend to harm us."

Harrington's device translated his words. A split-second later, Infinity heard a loud pop, and then three more. She then heard thuds behind her. She spun around to see four Marines sprawled on the ground, including Sergeant Harrington. Two of them weren't moving, while the other two were twitching with unmistakable death spasms.

"Jesus Christ," said Gideon. He quickly wheeled around and shot the nearest mounted lemur, knocking the creature from its vehicle.

The other robot fired two more times before the remaining Marines unleashed a barrage of projectiles and took out its rider.

Infinity rushed to Harrington and kneeled beside him. She knew he was dead before she even checked for a pulse. He had been shot in the face by a projectile at least an inch in diameter. Five other Marines lay motionless around him. Nearly half the squad had been wiped out in a matter of seconds.

Infinity sat back on her heels, trying to process their dwindling options. The remaining Marines were cursing and asking each other what the hell they were supposed to do next. Most of them were probably in their early twenties and were no doubt accustomed to following Harrington's orders. But now the sergeant was dead, and the current situation required immediate and decisive action.

Infinity rose to her feet. Several dozen lemur creatures were now gathered around the dead robot riders, and the crowd was growing.

"Listen," she said to the surviving humans. "We have two choices. We can run and try to find a place to hide, or we can surrender and hope for a chance to explain what—"

An amplified vocalization interrupted her. It was coming from one of the riderless vehicles. After speaking for several seconds, it fell silent, and Desmond's wrist device translated. "No weapons. You give to us weapons or we kill you now."

In perfect synchrony, both the robots took three steps toward the humans and stopped. The local lemur creatures backed away, giving the vehicles plenty of room.

Infinity now saw no other choice—they would have to

surrender. She spoke calmly. "Everyone put your weapons down. Show them that we're cooperating."

For several long seconds, no one moved.

"To hell with that!" one of the Marines said, and he fired at the robots.

A pop sounded and the Marine collapsed. Almost immediately, a second pop dropped another Marine.

"Run!" Infinity shouted.

The group turned en masse and sprinted east, directly away from the robots. Infinity heard another pop from behind, and a Marine no more than five feet to her right fell on his face.

"Evasives!" someone shouted.

The men started randomly zigzagging, making themselves more difficult targets. Infinity followed their lead and glanced over to make sure Desmond and Gideon were doing the same.

As the group rounded a shack, Infinity looked back over her shoulder. The vehicles didn't appear to be chasing them. Perhaps the machines weren't allowed to leave their riders behind, even though the riders were now dead. Had the robots acted on their own, or had they been taken over remotely after losing their riders? Either way, they had apparently decided to start slaughtering the humans.

The group kept running, weaving their way between the shacks of the seemingly endless shantytown. The remaining hints of twilight were giving way to darkness now, and they were seeing fewer of the lemur creatures moving around outside the dwellings. Eventually they slowed to a jog.

Desmond nudged Infinity's arm and pointed. "What is that, an outdoor theater?"

She stopped and looked. A few hundred yards to their left, a large rectangular screen displayed a video. Hundreds of spectators could be seen in the screen's glow, sitting on the ground. Abruptly, the crowd erupted with barks and whistles, apparently in response to something they'd just seen on the video.

Infinity turned her gaze to the screen. The image kept cutting away from one shot to another, but in the brief seconds of continuous video, it became apparent that a fight was taking place. Or more accurately, a pursuit was taking place, with moments of conflict followed by escape and then more pursuit. The pursuer was one of the lemur creatures, wearing a black body suit like those the spider riders had worn. The creature being pursued also appeared to be a lemur but without a body suit and with a white tail. All the lemurs Infinity had seen so far had brown tails.

The crowd erupted again as the black-clad lemur overtook its victim, and the two creatures tumbled into a vicious grappling fight.

"These bastards have a penchant for violence," Gideon said.

Infinity turned to see that Gideon had stopped beside her and Desmond. He was staring at the scene as well. He then tipped his head toward the Marines, who were still jogging ahead. "We'd better keep up. Not a good place to get separated."

Infinity glanced at the movie-watching crowd one more time and started running again, following Desmond, Gideon, and the Marines.

Eventually, after they had run at least a mile without seeing any of the creatures at all, they entered a wide field speckled with waist-high shrubs. Several hundred yards into the field, they finally stopped running. Infinity turned and looked back toward the shantytown. Faint lights were glowing from within thousands of shacks. Beyond the shacks, the high-rise structures of the city were solidly illuminated in brilliant colors, as if their exterior surfaces were glowing. She turned and looked in the direction they'd been running. Beyond the field of shrubs she could see nothing but the blackness of night.

"Shit!" one of the Marines sputtered while struggling to catch his breath. "What are we supposed to do now?"

"First," said Infinity, "let's get down so we're out of sight." She sat on the ground, and the others kneeled. The shrubs were sparse, but she was reasonably sure the group was far enough into the field to be concealed from the nearest shacks. She scanned the survivors who had made it to the field—Desmond, Gideon, and four Marines, their faces obscured by the darkness. "Who do we have left?" she asked.

"Corporal Vic Shepherd," said the Marine to her left. Shepherd was the one who had given Infinity, Desmond, and Gideon their sets of organic clothing.

"Private Terry Epsom," said the next guy over.

"Deon Lowman, private first class."

"Bishop Artliff, ma'am. Private."

Gideon cleared his throat softly. "I'm Gideon. Used to be a National Guardsman—specialist. Now I'm just a fellow human being, trying to save humanity."

"I'm Desmond Weaver. Bridger."

"And I'm Infinity. I'm a bridger too, if there's still such a thing."

"I emptied my weapon in the fight," Vic said, "so I tossed it a few miles back. Does anyone still have unfired projectiles?"

"I emptied mine during the first conflict and tossed it aside," said Deon.

"So did I," said Bishop.

Terry patted his gun. "I've got two left."

They all turned to Gideon. "I've, uh, only fired once. At

that son of a bitch robot rider that opened fire on us." He hesitated for a moment. "I didn't think it was necessary to kill until then."

Infinity addressed the whole group. "I have no idea what we're supposed to do now. We weren't given any rules for this goddamn test. Still, we have a job to do. We have to stop your world—which is now our world too—from being destroyed. I'm willing to bet getting killed isn't going to help us achieve that. So far, our encounters with the residents of this city have been disastrous. My opinion, for what it's worth, is that we should continue moving that way." She pointed into the dark unknown beyond the field.

"I agree," said Desmond. "For all we know, more robot riders are already searching for us. In fact, I'm surprised they haven't been searching for us from the air."

Infinity realized she hadn't seen any aircraft at all since they arrived. Strange, for a civilization advanced enough to have robot spider vehicles.

"Alright then," Vic said. "Let's keep moving until we find a place to hide until morning. Then we can decide on our next move."

Gideon and the remaining Marines nodded in agreement.

Without further discussion, the seven survivors got to their feet and headed east into the darkness.

8

———

MESH

APRIL 10 - 8:27 PM

DESMOND SLAPPED HIS CHEEK, trying to sharpen his focus. He'd lived through some intense, terrifying days over the last few years, but this one topped them all. In recent months, he had almost managed to forget what it felt like to constantly witness people dying all around him in horrible ways. He had grown to love his life on the arthropod world, and he was certain Infinity had been happy there too. But all of that was gone now—destroyed in less than a day. He just wanted to close his eyes and shut it all out. He was beyond exhausted. He slapped himself again, this time hitting his temple and scalp. He winced at the pain and felt wetness on his hand. He looked at it and realized his head was bleeding.

"Should I be concerned about you hitting yourself?" Infinity asked. She was walking beside him as the group made their way across the shrubby field.

"You didn't tell me I was bleeding."

"It looked superficial."

Knowing that Infinity's definition of *superficial* was quite different from his own, he felt the wound with his fingertips. She was right—the wound wasn't deep. He didn't even remember getting hit in the head. But he wouldn't soon forget the sight of a sentient, five-foot-tall lemur charging at him.

"I was wondering how long ago this world may have diverged from ours," he said.

"That's your department. Honestly, I don't give a musk monkey's ass. I just want to pass this stupid test and get the hell out of here."

Desmond knew better than to believe Infinity wasn't at all interested in their surroundings. She cared about everything that might have some bearing on survival, and she knew they had to survive or their new home world would be destroyed. He said, "The more we understand about this world, the better chance we have of passing the test."

She sighed. "Alright then. When do you suppose the two worlds diverged?"

"Depends whether I'm right about what type of creatures these are. I could be wrong, but they look to me to be descended from prosimians—primitive primates, like lemurs or lorises, or maybe tarsiers."

"I've already started calling them lemurs," she said.

He felt the urge to smile, in spite of his exhaustion. "So have I, actually, although their enormous eyes remind me more of tarsiers. But let's say they are direct descendants of prosimians. If so, then this world must have diverged from ours before the appearance of simians—monkeys and apes."

She huffed a brief laugh. "Because if simians had existed and had become sentient, they would have wiped out any other creatures that had the bad manners to develop their own intelligence."

He glanced at her in the darkness. "Well, yes. But that's a cynical way to put it."

She shrugged. "Humans are simians, right?"

"Yeah."

"Then I'm just being truthful. We wipe out anything that tries to become as powerful as us. Hell, all intelligent species do it. Think about the Outlanders. Think about Kitty, Tigger, and Teddy—their whole species. They wipe out entire civilizations because they don't like the way they use technology. In case you haven't noticed, the only survivors from our own version of Earth are you, me, Gideon, and a few others who are now on a world that's about to be destroyed if we fail here. This goddamn trial could cause our extinction."

Desmond realized Infinity was as exhausted as he was. Exhaustion tended to bring out her fatalistic side. He reached out and squeezed her hand before going on. "Anyway, as I was saying, it seems unlikely that any of the prosimians could have evolved to such a level of intelligence if the apes or monkeys had been around at the same time. Which means there's a good chance this world diverged from ours forty to sixty million years ago, before the simians appeared."

"Maybe," she said. "But I can see another possibility. Lemurs came from Madagascar, right? They were isolated there. Maybe on this world the lemurs in Madagascar became intelligent within the last few million years. Then they could have spread out across the planet and wiped out all the humans. Or at least the ancestors of humans."

Desmond considered this. "Huh, you're right, that is a possibility. It hadn't even occured to me."

She reached over and tapped his scalp. "Maybe you should quit smacking yourself in the head."

"What is that?" one of the Marines said, pointing straight ahead.

Desmond followed his gaze and saw it immediately—a tall, looming darkness. It appeared to be a forest. The group fell silent as they drew nearer. The closer they got to the forest, the taller the shadowy trees became. At about fifty yards out, Desmond had to crane his neck to see the canopy. These trees were taller than any he'd ever seen. He could now hear a variety of monotonous calls coming from within the forest, possibly from frogs or insects, or from creatures unlike any he'd ever known.

Gideon spoke, his voice coming from about thirty yards ahead. "There's a barrier here, a fence of some kind. I almost ran into it."

The group converged beside Gideon. Before them was a mesh fence, with square openings about five inches wide. Desmond reached out and touched the mesh. It felt softer than wire—perhaps some kind of plastic. The barrier was too tall for him to be able to see the top in the dark. It could be twenty feet high, or it could be taller than the trees themselves, which he estimated were at least 150 feet.

"The best place for us to hide is in the forest," Infinity said. "Which means we need to get over this fence."

Desmond frowned. He couldn't help but remember another fence, one that he and Infinity had encountered on a different version of Earth. That fence, it turned out, had been constructed for a very good reason—to protect the diminutive villagers, thirdlings, from a much larger hominid species, the orcs. To say that the orcs were aggressive would be a monumental understatement.

"We have no idea what's in that forest," he said, hoping Infinity would understand his concern.

"Yeah, well, we do know what's on *this* side of the fence," Vic Shepherd said. "What could be worse than killer lemurs riding killer robots?"

"There are plenty of things that could be worse," Desmond replied.

Vic ignored him and rubbed his hands together. "Okay, I'm gonna try climbing over." He started making his way up the fence, and seconds later his receding shape disappeared into the darkness above.

The remaining six stood in silence, listening to the orchestra of animal calls as they waited for Vic to give them a report.

"Ow, shit!" he cried out from far above.

Vic's body didn't come falling down, so Desmond—and apparently the others—assumed he wasn't seriously hurt. They continued waiting until they saw the Marine climbing back down the mesh.

Vic dropped the last few feet to the ground and turned around. "There ain't no climbing over. The top of the fence curves out toward this side and then down. As if that ain't enough, the mesh on that top part is charged with something. Didn't feel like no electric shock, but it started getting hot wherever I touched it. I had to let go after a few seconds."

"This fence isn't very well maintained," said Gideon, who was now about twenty yards or so to the right. "Over here— there's a hole."

They all moved to where he was kneeling. The hole was at ground level. It was perhaps large enough for a medium-sized dog, but not an adult human. Gideon grabbed the mesh and lifted, grunting with the effort. This doubled the opening's size.

"What do you think?" asked Deon, "Should we go through?".

"Based on the design up top," said Vic, "the fence was made to keep these lemur people on this side. So its purpose ain't for keeping dangerous animals out of the city. Suppose I could be wrong, though."

Infinity nodded toward the forest. "The trees will provide good cover. It's been a hell of a day. Maybe you guys are rested enough, but I'm reaching the point where my judgement is screwed up. We need to try to get some sleep, and we can't do it out here in the open."

"Fair enough," Vic said. "How many votes for going under the fence and holing up in the trees?"

Everyone but Desmond grunted in agreement. Desmond stared through the mesh. If he'd had any hairs left on the back of his neck, the thought of entering the inky-black woods would have made them stand on end. But what other choice did they have? He sighed. "Okay, let's do it."

Desmond pictured Kitty sitting in her pod beneath the ground, watching their every move. What would she think of them taking a democratic vote on whether to crawl under the fence? Would she consider such behavior a strength or a weakness? What if she had already decided, based on their recent actions, that the human species didn't deserve to exist? Maybe she had already bridged back and had activated the green cones of destruction, leaving Desmond and the others here to die.

Gideon raised the mesh again, and the other members of the team crawled through, one at a time. Desmond got on his belly and wormed his way under the fence. Once he was through, he got up and held the mesh for Gideon. Seconds later they were all standing in a cluster, staring into the darkness.

"You bridgers have more experience with this wilderness stuff," Vic said. "Any advice?"

Infinity pointed to the hole they'd just come through. "We might need to use that opening as an escape route. I suggest we stay near it. We should move into the forest just far enough to be hidden from view if the lemurs come searching for us."

"We'll just have to hope they don't use heat signature detectors or tracking animals," Gideon added. "For all we know, they might actually *be* tracking animals, with sensitive noses."

"Anything else?" Vic asked.

Infinity said, "Don't get killed."

They pushed their way through the thick vegetation at the forest's edge, which quickly gave way to a more open interior.

"I don't think we need to go any farther than this," Desmond whispered when they were about ten yards into the forest. It was impossible to know how good the lemurs' eyesight was, but it seemed like, with the humans concealed by both the darkness and the thick vegetation, the creatures would be unable to spot them from the other side of the fence. Just as important, it seemed reasonable to assume large predators would stay a good distance away from the fence.

"Agreed," Infinity said. She turned to the Marines. "Have any of you slept in a tree before?"

The Marines looked at each other. "Can't say I've ever had cause to do so," Terry said.

"Then let's take our chances on the ground," she said. "We can stand watch in shifts, about an hour each."

"I'll take first shift, then," Vic said. "I'll stay on my feet so I don't crash out."

The seven survivors quickly decided the order in which they'd stand watch. Then everyone but Vic settled in, evenly spaced around the base of a massive tree, with their backs against the trunk.

As the group quieted down, Desmond focused on the ground around his legs, listening for skittering bugs and waiting for small creatures to start crawling on his skin.

Surprisingly, he hadn't yet been bitten by any mosquitoes or other insects. It was possible they didn't even exist on this world, but that was probably wishful thinking.

Infinity was sitting to his right, and she placed a hand on his thigh. He put his hand on her hand. He then formed words in his mind and projected them outward, visualizing them speeding down his arm, passing from his hand to hers, and then moving up her arm to her brain. "You hanging in there?"

She jerked with surprise, as she usually did when he used his thought-projection ability without warning her first. But then she squeezed his hand, letting him know she wasn't giving up.

He continued projecting his thoughts. "I know we've lost our home again. But I swear, if we live through this trial, we're going to find a new home. Some place where we can live the rest of our lives together without fear of the entire planet imploding. When we get there, I promise we will never bridge again."

She squeezed his hand again. Then she leaned toward him and whispered in his ear. "You know what? We may soon go down with the rest of our species. That sucks. But at least I'll die fighting beside you." She inched closer and bit down on his earlobe, just hard enough to send a wave of tingles through his entire body. She pulled back and settled in again, shifting her shoulders to find a comfortable position.

Desmond considered his promise to her. At this point, it seemed unlikely he'd ever have a chance to keep it. But he had learned not to underestimate Infinity's resourcefulness—and his own, for that matter. Perhaps they'd live long enough to stumble upon an opportunity to show Kitty and her species that humans deserved to exist. He tried imagining what that opportunity might look like, but then he felt his mind shutting down and he gave in to sleep.

————————

Someone shook Desmond's shoulder. He forced his eyes open, trying to remember where he was. It was no longer dark. Inches from his face were the fearful eyes of one of the Marines, Bishop Artliff. Bishop's finger was pressed to his own lips, signaling Desmond to be silent.

"We have company," the Marine whispered, barely loud enough to be heard. He pointed upward.

Desmond wiped his eyes, looked up, and squinted. At first he saw only green vegetation and a few pinpoints of sunlight shining through. But then he spotted it—a figure crouched on a limb. Was it a person? No, it had a bushy tail hanging below its body. The tail was striking, with alternating rings of black and tan fur, like the tail of a raccoon or a ring-tailed lemur. In fact, the creature looked very similar to the lemurs that inhabited the city, but this one was clearly a completely different species. Desmond estimated it weighed about a hundred pounds, smaller than the city-dwelling lemurs. But its eyes were even larger, at least three inches across. The creature was resting on a branch about fifteen yards above the ground, staring down at the humans.

Bishop crept to the side, gently shook Infinity awake, and pointed to the lemur. She spotted the creature and nodded.

Bishop moved on to rouse Gideon, and Desmond began scanning the other trees above. He quickly spotted a second lemur, and then a third. All of them were of the same species, and they were all staring intently at the humans. Unlike the lemurs in the city, these creatures wore no clothing. Were they merely wild animals that hadn't developed sentient intelligence? It certainly seemed like their huge eyeballs wouldn't leave much room in the skull for a well-developed cerebrum.

Desmond slowly got to his feet, keeping his eyes on the creatures. In his peripheral vision he saw Gideon start to raise his weapon but then lower it as Infinity pushed it back down with her hand. Desmond smiled up at the nearest lemur without showing his teeth, hoping this wouldn't be interpreted as a challenge or an insult.

The creatures watched him without moving.

He took a deep breath, let it out, and spoke. "Hello. We hope you don't mind us being here."

The creatures all raised their heads at once, becoming more alert. One of them let out a bark, followed by a series of rapid trills and whistles. This was answered by another lemur, and then by another that Desmond hadn't even noticed. This call-and-response pattern continued, eliciting calls from one lemur after another. Desmond spun around as the answers multiplied, gradually realizing that he and the other humans were surrounded by at least ten of the creatures.

The vocalizations abruptly stopped, and the lemur that had spoken first descended its tree, landed lightly on the ground, and rose to its full height, nearly five feet tall. It then approached Desmond, walking on its hind legs, its splendid tail bobbing up and down conspicuously. When it was standing about five feet away, it spoke again, rattling off a complex series of nonhuman sounds.

The humans' translators remained silent. These creatures must have been speaking a different language than that used by the city lemurs.

As Desmond tried to decide on his next move, the other creatures descended from their trees and gathered around the humans in a semicircle.

The other humans got to their feet. Desmond glanced at

Gideon and Terry, the only two who still had weapons. "Please don't start shooting unless they actually attack, okay?"

Desmond's words prompted another round of chattering from the lemurs. He raised his brows at Gideon and Terry. Both men nodded, keeping their weapons pointed at the ground.

Desmond's translator spoke abruptly. "Confusion. Fear."

The creatures paused and stared at Desmond's wrist.

"I guess that's better than violence and anger," Infinity said.

The creatures started chattering again, and Desmond raised his arm to make sure his translator picked up as much speech as possible.

"Confusion, fear, curiosity," the device said.

Again the creatures fell silent. One of them stepped forward, staring at the translator but glancing up frequently at Desmond's face as if watching for signs that he might attack.

"This device is a translator," Desmond said, pointing to his wrist. "When you talk, it learns your language. Using this translator, we can talk to you, and you can talk to us."

The translator emitted a sequence of sounds, already attempting to translate his words into the lemurs' language.

The creatures froze, staring at the device. When the translator fell silent again, every pair of three-inch eyes flicked from the translator to Desmond's face.

Everyone was silent for several long seconds. Finally, the lemur directly in front of Desmond spoke. After the creature was finished, the translator spoke. "You new here. This our place. Why you here?"

Desmond turned and met Infinity's gaze.

"Don't look at me," she said. "You know I'm terrible with negotiations. Say whatever you think needs to be said."

"Yeah, you go for it, Desmond," Vic said.

The translators remained silent, apparently somehow aware that these words were not directed at the lemurs.

Desmond turned back to the creatures. "We didn't want to be here. We know we don't belong here." He pointed toward the fence. "The city dwellers attacked us. We had to come here."

His device translated his words for the lemurs.

Another one of the creatures spoke up—a long, complex series of precise sounds.

Desmond's device took a few seconds to process the lemur's speech and then said, "Yes, city dwellers attack. City dwellers always attack. That is why city dwellers put us here. They put us here. Each day they come here and attack. They kill. They attack for fun. They kill for fun. Now you here. They attack you. They kill you. They attack and kill you for fun."

Desmond stared at the creatures, not wanting to believe what he had just heard.

"Shit," Vic muttered.

9

———

HAPPY

APRIL 11 - 6:51 AM

INFINITY CONSIDERED the words Desmond's translator had just spoken. Something didn't make sense. She scanned the foliage until she found the fence. In the daylight, she could now see enough of the fence to confirm that Vic had been correct—the fence was designed to keep the city dwellers out of the forest, not to keep things from the forest out of the city.

Desmond spoke to the creatures again. "Why do the city dwellers attack and kill you?"

After the translation, the creature that had first spoken responded, its round eyes blinking frequently as it spoke. Desmond's translator said, "City dwellers attack and kill for fun. Attack and kill is honor for city dwellers. Wealthy city dwellers attack and kill. Honor for wealthy city dwellers only."

So maybe the forest was a hunting preserve set aside for the rich, and the fence was just to keep out the riffraff.

"You are different," Desmond's translator continued. "We want to know what you are."

"Yes, we are different," he replied. "We are from a very different place. We come from far away."

"But you are intelligent. You talk. Nine different types of beings are intelligent. Not ten. Only nine. You are not one of the nine species of intelligent beings."

"Wait, there are nine species of intelligent beings on this world?" Desmond asked.

"Yes, nine. Not ten. You are not one of the nine. We want to know what you are."

Desmond glanced at Infinity as if unsure of how much he should say.

She just shrugged.

He sighed. "We are not one of the nine on this world because we came here from another world. We came from a world that only has one type of intelligent being."

The lemurs listened to the translation and then chattered back and forth without taking their eyes off the humans. The translators remained silent. Finally, the crowd quieted down and the center lemur spoke. This time Desmond's device responded. "Yes, the city dwellers talk of going to other worlds. The city dwellers talk of going to other worlds to find other intelligent beings. They talk of bringing other intelligent beings to this world. They talk of putting intelligent beings into enclosures like our enclosure and attacking and killing the intelligent beings. For honor. For fun."

Infinity had already disliked the city dwellers. Now she despised them. She spoke to the other humans. "It sounds like this lemur is suggesting the city dwellers have access to bridging technology."

"Maybe they found the Outlanders' signal," Terry said.

Desmond shook his head. "Not likely. The Outlanders

transmitted their signal tens of thousands of years ago. I'm pretty sure this universe diverged from ours long before that, perhaps tens of *millions* of years ago. There's almost no chance the Outlanders exist at all in this universe."

Terry furrowed his hairless brow. "Well, maybe the city lemurs developed bridging technology themselves. Maybe they didn't need the Outlanders' signal."

"Not a chance," Infinity said. "A species that can't solve problems like extreme poverty and piles of trash couldn't be smart enough to develop bridging technology without help."

"Maybe the wealthy just don't care about the quality of life in poor areas." Desmond suggested.

Abruptly, the lemurs all whipped their heads around and looked toward the fence. Infinity felt her muscles tighten. She didn't see or hear anything unusual, but these creatures obviously did.

The center lemur turned back to the humans and rattled off some trills and whistles. Desmond's translator said, "City dwellers are near. City dwellers have vehicles. Probably they are looking for you. Do you wish them to find you, or do you wish to hide?"

"What will happen if the city dwellers find us?" Infinity asked.

The lemur listened to the translation and then responded. "City dwellers attack and kill. City dwellers always attack and kill. For honor. For fun."

"Then we wish to hide," she said.

The lemur listened to the translation and then spoke again. "They are coming nearer. Probably they are following evidence that you left behind when you came here. You must hide now or they will attack and kill you. We want to know more about what you are, and so we will help you hide."

Infinity could now hear a chittering sound coming from beyond the fence. "Yes, please help us."

The creature stepped closer and slowly reached out a hand. It took one of Desmond's hands in its own and gazed at it. The lemur's slender fingers were at least twice the length of Desmond's. It spoke, and Desmond's translator said, "Are you not able to climb and move in the trees?"

Desmond shook his head. "No, we are ground-dwelling creatures."

The lemur released his hand. "I see that this is true."

The chittering was getting louder, and Infinity's legs were beginning to twitch as she fought the urge to run. She was about to say something when the lemurs all turned in unison and began briskly walking. They kept going without looking back.

"I guess we're supposed to follow them," Vic said.

The group took off walking after the lemurs. Before long they had to start jogging to keep up, dodging trees and shoving aside low vegetation.

The lemurs remained silent as the group made steady progress. The humans followed their lead and remained quiet as well.

After following the lemurs for about a half mile, Infinity saw an open area ahead where sunlight was breaking through the forest canopy. As the group approached the open area, Infinity noticed that the air in the clearing appeared to be moving. At first she thought she might be seeing smoke, but soon she realized the movement was from thousands upon thousands of winged insects, rising and falling in mesmerizing waves.

The lemurs led the humans directly into the clearing. Before Infinity had even stepped out of the forest's shadows into the light, she could hear the buzzing of countless wings.

The clearing was about two hundred yards across and was filled with shoulder-high plants bursting with red and yellow flowers, arranged in cultivated rows.

Infinity paused, looking out over the vast field of flowers. She could hardly see the far side through the cloud of insects. It was like looking through a blizzard. Something moved in one of the gaps between rows—an object had popped up briefly and then disappeared. There was another to the right, and then another to the left. She moved forward and looked down the long gap between two of the rows, where she saw a ring-tail lemur darting about, swinging what appeared to be an insect net. After several more swipes of the net, the creature paused and emptied the net's contents into a satchel hanging from its neck by a strap. It then went back to swooping up insects, apparently oblivious to the humans passing by.

In the next gap over, Infinity found two more of the insect-catching lemurs. One of them noticed her and stopped what it was doing and stared. It then emitted a loud, chittering whistle, and both the lemurs in the row came running.

Infinity instinctively took a defensive stance as the two lemurs came charging at her. Before long, dozens of others were pouring out of the rows and gathering around. The humans were surrounded by creatures wielding insect nets and satchels full of buzzing bugs. Barks, chirps, and whistles filled the air as the gathering crowd chattered with the lemurs that had been leading the humans. Infinity wished she could understand what they were saying, but the translators only seemed to work when someone was directly addressing a being who spoke a different language.

The group moved on, leaving the insect gatherers chattering amongst themselves. Infinity took one last look at the rows of flowers before the lemurs led the humans into the murky forest again. They hadn't walked more than a hundred yards when they came upon another odd sight. On the forest floor, hundreds of logs were arranged side by side in rows. The logs were in various stages of decomposition, and a few dozen lemurs were busy pulling apart the older, softer logs and plucking insects from the debris. Like the other insect gatherers, these lemurs were also depositing their harvest into satchels.

"Impressive," Desmond said. "The insects must be a food source."

"I'm hungry," Infinity said. "I wouldn't turn down a bug meal if they offered it." She had gotten used to eating giant arthropods during the last nineteen months. It was just a difference in scale.

This new group of insect gatherers spotted the newcomers, prompting another round of excited chattering between the workers and the humans' guides.

Once the caravan was moving again, the lemurs led the way through another field of flowering plants and two more rotting log stations, all of which were being worked by satchel-bearing gatherers. Then the group passed through an area where lemurs were busy hacking tree limbs down to various lengths, creating poles that were probably useful for construction. The creatures were using sharpened rocks to do this, and Infinity noted the distinct contrast between these crude tools and the gleaming towers and high-tech materials Infinity had seen in the city beyond the fence. Apparently these lemurs were much more primitive than the city dwellers.

After passing the log-cutting station, the lemur guides finally stopped and turned to the humans. One of the creatures began speaking. Vic was closest to the creature, and his translator was the one that responded. "We soon will be at our home. The city dwellers do not come to our home. We will let you hide at our home. We will have talking and questions. We want to know more. We want to know what you are and where you have come from."

As Infinity listened to Vic's translator, she gazed at the lemur who had spoken. An old, healed scar ran from its chin to its ear. Other than that, there were few differences between this individual and all the others. Perhaps to each other these creatures were as distinctive as humans were to other humans, but Infinity was finding it difficult to tell the lemurs apart. She did notice four nipples—two high and two low—on Scarface's abdomen, as well as on several of the others, apparently females. The nipples were each about the size and shape of a human pinky toe. But otherwise, Infinity could see no differences between the males and females.

Infinity looked directly at Scarface. "Why are you allowing us to hide at your home?"

The female lemur listened to the translation and then replied, "I have told you. We want to know what you are." She paused as the translation finished. Even then she seemed to hesitate before going on. "Maybe we can help you. If the city dwellers have brought you here so that they can attack you and kill you for honor and for fun, maybe we can teach you. Maybe we can teach you, and you can go to the enclosure where the city dwellers have put the others of your species. You can teach the others of your species what we have taught you, so you and the others like you will not die. Maybe you will live happy, as we live happy."

Infinity glanced at Desmond and then at Gideon. Both were frowning.

Desmond spoke to Scarface. "It's just us. There aren't any others like us."

After the translation, the lemurs chattered to each other for at least a full minute. Scarface then turned to Desmond and spoke. This time it was Desmond's translator that responded. "The words you speak are troubling. We are surprised. We don't understand. We see only seven of you. If there aren't any others like you, the city dwellers will not be able to attack you and kill you for honor and for fun. We think they intend to make more of you. They will force you to make more of your species. They will force you to make babies. If you are the only ones like you, they will want to find you. They will work very much to find you."

Another of the female lemurs pointed directly at Infinity and spoke. When she was finished, Infinity's translator said, "I believe you are female and the others are male. I am surprised. I don't understand. If the city dwellers want you to make babies, why did they take only one female?"

Infinity let out a frustrated growl. "The city dwellers didn't take us! And they didn't bring us here. We came to this world on our own. We're from a different world, and we're just trying to stay alive long enough to do whatever we're supposed to do, so we can go home."

The creatures listened and then talked amongst themselves again. After a few moments, they fell silent, and Scarface spoke. "What are you supposed to do, so you can go home?"

Infinity was getting tired of this conversation—it wasn't going anywhere. "That's the problem. We don't know what we're supposed to do. But look—we appreciate you letting us hide from the city dwellers. Thank you. We'd be happy to answer any questions you have about us."

The lemurs listened to the translation and then chatted again. The individual that had annoyingly pointed out that Infinity was female addressed the humans again. "We will take you to our home. We will have water and food for you. We will have shelter and comfort for you. We will learn more about you. Then you must go. If the city dwellers know you are in our enclosure, they will find you. They will come to our home. We do not want them to come to our home. They will find you, and they will force you to make babies, and they will put you in your own enclosure. Once there are more of you, they will attack you and kill you for honor and for fun. We will teach you before you go. We will teach you how to live happy. You can live happy even when the city dwellers attack and kill one of you every day."

The lemurs all turned simultaneously and began walking again.

"Every day?" Gideon said as the group resumed following. "You really think those bastards come in here and kill one of these guys every day?"

"Maybe this is our trial," Desmond said. "Maybe Kitty wants to see if we have enough compassion to help these beings."

Infinity doubted this was the case. She was about to respond when Deon said, "I didn't get the impression Kitty and her pals were big on compassion."

Infinity glanced at the weapons Gideon and Terry were still gripping at their sides. "You guys hold on to those guns. If those goddamn city lemurs really do come in here after us, let's at least make sure we kill as many as we can."

The two men nodded silently.

10

PERFORMANCE

APRIL 11 - 8:19 AM

THE RING-TAIL LEMURS' home was not at all what Desmond had imagined it would be. He had envisioned a collection of filthy hovels with a few dozen lemurs eking out a primitive existence, surviving despite being relentlessly hunted and killed by the city dwellers. Instead, before him was a thriving village large enough to house hundreds of ring-tails. The dwellings and other structures were certainly rustic, made mostly of sticks and woven plant fibers, but unlike the shacks Desmond had seen at the edge of the city, these dwellings were well kept. They were also cleverly decorated with colorful items that likely had been pilfered from the piles of trash in the shantytown. Which could explain the hole in the fence.

About half the dwellings had been built on the ground, arranged in clusters around the bases of large trees. The other half were built at various heights in the trees, using branches for support, the lowest no more than ten feet up, and the highest, astoundingly, at least a hundred feet above the ground. Just staring up at the higher dwellings made Desmond dizzy.

As the humans entered the village, a sizable crowd of chattering ring-tails gathered around. Desmond nearly had to cover his ears from the noise. He felt like he was surrounded simultaneously by barking dogs and squawking parrots. The lemurs were either excited or distressed—Desmond couldn't tell the difference. Their eyes were always perfectly round, making it nearly impossible to read their facial expressions. While their barks, whistles, and clicks were more rapid than usual, Desmond's translator was silent, giving no clues about what they were saying.

This chaotic discussion went on for several minutes before the crowd began pulling back to give the humans room. But even then Desmond was uncomfortably aware of the hundreds of eyes watching him and his companions. So far, these beings seemed friendly, but what if the humans inadvertently insulted them or violated some social norm? To complicate matters, the humans were speaking through translators, which were no doubt delivering imperfect translations.

As they were led through throngs of onlooking ring-tails, Desmond was surprised that the entire village smelled pleasant. It took him a moment to realize it, but the most prominent smell was that of honey, or at least something similar.

As the group passed by one of the dwellings, Desmond was again struck by the structure's simple but aesthetically appealing design. These creatures were clearly more intelligent than the apparent lack of technology in their village would suggest. The only explanation Desmond could think of was that the ring-tails were being forced to live this way. Which was consistent with what they had told the humans so far.

The group finally stopped in a clearing, which seemed to be the center of the village. Desmond estimated the crowd to now be over six hundred, and more were still coming. The lemurs' excited chattering was becoming unbearably noisy.

Frustrated that his translator was doing nothing, Desmond held the device to his face and said, "What are they talking about?"

To his surprise, the device actually responded. "Confusion. Excitement. Occasionally fear."

Infinity looked over at him. "Did your translator just talk back to you?"

He nodded and spoke up so she could hear. "Who knew?"

A shrill whistle sounded, and the crowd became hushed. Desmond spotted the creature that made the noise, a male ring-tail with gray hairs amidst the fur on his head, neck, and face. The creature had several patches of bare, pink skin on his shoulders and chest, which appeared to be the result of old scars. He was standing beside the female lemur Infinity had been referring to as Scarface. Desmond decided to call this one Grayface.

Grayface pointed at the humans. He then emitted a long series of sounds. Terry was nearest to the creature, and his translator responded. "I have been told that you have devices that translate your language to ours and our language to yours. Your devices interest us. We want to know more about your devices. But first we want to know more about you. We do not know what you are. You have said you are from another world. You are not one of the nine intelligent species of this world, and therefore you must indeed be from another world. We want to know more. Tell us more. We will listen and learn."

Desmond glanced at his companions. They were all looking at him as if they assumed speaking to the lemurs was his job. "Me?" He sighed. "Alright, well, feel free to jump in if

I leave anything out. Also, unless you can think of a reason I shouldn't, I'm going to tell them the truth—why we're here and how we got here."

Most of the group responded with nods or shrugs. Infinity said, "We have no way of knowing whether telling the truth will help us or hurt us, assuming Kitty's even still watching."

Desmond turned to Grayface and began telling his story. Every few sentences, he stopped to allow for translation, holding his wrist device up so the lemurs could hear. He first described how the humans of his own version of Earth had discovered the Outlanders' instructions for building bridging devices. He explained that those devices had completely destroyed his version of Earth. As he neared the part of the story where the mongrels had given him the key needed to unlock the true powers of bridging technology, he considered leaving out any mention of the key, for fear that Kitty would see this as a violation of the rules. But at the last moment he decided to include it. After all, Kitty and her people only seemed concerned about giving the key away, not about mentioning its existence. At least Desmond hoped this was the case.

He skipped over the nineteen months his colony had been living on the arthropod world and went straight to telling about the unexpected arrival of Kitty, Tigger, and Teddy, and the trial they had forced upon the humans. He finished the story by explaining that he and his companions were now being watched, and that if they didn't pass Kitty's mysterious test, they would be killed along with billions of other humans.

The ring-tails had been surprisingly quiet and attentive throughout his story, but as soon as he stated that he was done, the crowd erupted with chattering. Grayface whistled again to quiet them down. He then spoke directly to Desmond, and Desmond's translator said, "We are interested in your bridging device. We understand that you cannot give us the key. The key would not help us anyway. We would not be able to build a bridging device. The city dwellers allow us to build, but only the simplest of structures, and with simple tools. We are interested in using *your* bridging device."

This took Desmond by surprise, and he turned to the others for help.

Infinity shook her head. "Not a chance in hell."

"Ask them why they want to use it," Vic said.

Desmond turned to ask the question, but his translator went ahead and spoke in the ring-tail language, apparently understanding the nature of Vic's request.

Grayface listened and then replied without hesitation. "We are interested in using your bridging device because we want to go away. We will go to another world. We will go to a world without the city dwellers. We will then live happy. We will not be attacked and killed every day. We will build our own cities, as we did long ago."

"Well, crap," Desmond muttered. He had been hoping for a way to help these creatures, but now he was starting to realize the hopelessness of their situation.

Infinity stepped forward and addressed Grayface. "How many of you are there?"

The lemur listened and then replied. "Today we have eight hundred seven. However, there will be a hunt this afternoon, and perhaps it will be a kill."

Infinity turned to Desmond and raised her brows.

Desmond thought for a moment. The logistics seemed daunting, but not impossible. He had been directly involved in bridging out colonies of 712 people each while his planet was dying, and that had been without the enhanced bridging abilities made possible by the key. "Maybe this is how we prove ourselves to Kitty," he said. He suspected he was wrong about this, but anything was worth trying.

Vic stepped forward. "You guys can't be serious. How would we even—"

Grayface interjected with another stream of speech, and Desmond's device translated. "There are also other groups of our species, held in enclosures near each of the city dwellers' cities. We do not know how many cities they have, but we estimate twenty-four hundred ninety-three. Each group of our species is probably equal in size to our group. We are interested in bringing all of our species to another world. There are also groups of seven other intelligent species held in the enclosures around each of the city dwellers' cities. They too are attacked and killed every day. We are interested in bringing the seven other intelligent species to a new world with us. They will build their own cities, as they did long ago. It will be a world of happy living."

Infinity flopped her head back and growled. She stared up toward the forest canopy for a moment and then lowered her head and leveled her gaze at Desmond. "Okay, scratch that. Any other ideas for how we can prove ourselves?"

He wasn't ready to give up on the idea yet. "Of course we can't save them all. But that didn't stop us from evacuating a few human colonies from our Earth. Saving some is better than saving none. And it still might be a way we can prove ourselves worthy."

She rolled her eyes and turned away, having obviously decided saving these lemurs was impossible. Desmond knew deep down it probably *was* impossible, but he also wanted to believe that Kitty was looking for behaviors that proved humans were honorable and compassionate. Kitty's people had sent him and his group of humans to a world of unthinkable cruelty and oppression—probably not a random destination. It just seemed logical to Desmond that his group was expected to help these creatures.

"Reality check," Gideon said. "How in the hell would we bridge *any* of these creatures out of here? We can't even bridge ourselves out."

Desmond shook his head. "I don't know!" But then an idea came to him. He tapped the tiny bump on his forehead where the camera was embedded. "Kitty? Are you listening? We want to bridge these lemur people to another world. The city dwellers are murdering them every day, and we want to help them escape. But we're going to need your assistance." He waited a moment. "Can you hear me?"

Nothing. No surprise there.

The wrist translators had remained silent while the humans discussed what to do. Grayface and the other lemurs had been watching patiently, apparently fascinated by the unintelligible speech of a species they'd never encountered before. They stared, still transfixed by the humans, as Desmond waited for a response from Kitty.

"Well then," Infinity said after several seconds of silence. She turned to Grayface. "We would like to help you, but it's not possible for any of us to use the bridging device." Just as her translator finished, and before Grayface could reply, she said, "And I have to pee. I have to urinate." She made a dispersal motion with her hand near her crotch. "I haven't done it since last night. Also, since the others are probably too polite to ask, do you have any water we could drink?"

INFINITY WASN'T the only one about to burst. Desmond was nearly to the point of having to dance to keep from leaking into his organic pants. When the translator had finished,

Grayface responded by escorting the humans to a row of thirteen structures no more than fifty yards away that could only be described as outhouses. Each structure was made primarily of tree branches but with colorful scrap items integrated into the doors and outer walls. The scrap items appeared to be pieces of trash from the other side of the fence—trash that didn't look much different from what one might have found in a landfill back on Desmond's own version of Earth. Some of the items appeared to be molded plastic, while others were metal or wood.

Desmond opened the door to one of the outhouses, expecting to be hit by the stench that is typical of outhouses. Instead, his nostrils filled with the aroma of honey. Did these creatures actually crap out honey? The first thing he noticed inside the structure was a round seat that looked to be made from a hollow section of a tree trunk, about eight inches high and polished smooth. Perhaps this was the lemurs' optimal squatting height. Through the hole in the center of the seat, he could see and hear water flowing by from left to right below. Apparently the ring-tails had diverted a stream into an underground tunnel and then placed all thirteen of the outhouses in a row above the aqueduct.

Desmond's organic trousers had no fly, so he had to pull on the waistline until they had loosened enough for him to pull them down. As he peed into the hole, he gazed around at the inside of the outhouse. He didn't see anything resembling toilet paper, and he was grateful that he only had to urinate.

After the humans had all finished their business, they were led back to the center of the clearing. Several lemurs were in the process of placing hundreds of green, heart-shaped leaves on the ground, each about twelve inches wide. Many of the others were settling into seated positions with the leaves in front of them, their heels against their butts and knees on either side of their chins. While about half of the villagers got seated, the other half busily prepared for what was beginning to look like a communal meal. Grayface instructed the humans to sit in the center of the clearing. They complied, sitting cross-legged, surrounded by hundreds of seated lemurs.

A ring-tail approached, carrying a thick stack of leaves, and placed one in front of each human. Dozens of lemurs emerged from one of the dwellings carrying wide trays that appeared to be made of leather stretched across rectangular frameworks of wood. The leather sagged beneath the weight of a dark substance that was heaped high on each tray.

A pair of the lemurs, carrying a single tray between them, came directly to the seated humans. They lowered the tray in front of Desmond, and the scent of honey filled his nostrils yet again. One of the lemurs spoke, and Desmond's translator said, "This is food for your body. You eat this food, and your body will be fast and strong so that you can serve your people with honor. Take as much of the food as you can eat."

Desmond glanced out at the crowd of seated lemurs and saw one of the creatures using a wooden utensil to scoop food from a tray onto its own leaf. A thought occurred to him—this food was specifically suited to the dietary needs of the lemurs. What if it made him and the other humans sick?

Some of the lemurs around him seemed to be watching and waiting patiently, so he plucked the spatula-shaped utensil from the tray and scooped a glob of the stuff onto his leaf. He put the utensil back. While the others were scooping their own portions, he leaned forward and studied the substance on his leaf. Not surprisingly, it smelled strongly of sweet nectar or honey, although it was much darker in color than honey. He poked the stuff with his finger and realized suddenly why its color was so dark—it was filled with mashed insects. Legs, antennae, and bits of exoskeleton darkened the otherwise translucent substance. He scooped some up with his finger and tasted it, finding it to be just as sweet as its aroma.

"It's better than it looks," he said to the four Marines, who appeared far less enthusiastic. "And it should be safe to eat. Gideon, Infinity, and I have been living on a diet of arthropods for a year and a half without ill effects."

"Arthropods," Vic repeated dryly. "You're talking about bugs." He took a small taste from his fingertip.

Infinity spoke around a mouthful of the substance. "We don't know how long we'll be here. You should eat."

Grayface, one of the few lemurs still on his feet, approached the humans and spoke. Desmond's translator said, "We believe that you possess weapons. We would like to know what you intend to do with your weapons. Do you intend to harm us?"

Gideon surprised Desmond by speaking up first. "We brought weapons to protect ourselves." He held up his gun with the muzzle pointed straight down. "We won't use them unless we are attacked. You have been kind to us, so we do not want to harm you."

Grayface listened to Gideon's translator and then replied. "We would like to introduce to you our young. Our children. However, we will not introduce to you our children until you have given us your weapons. We will return your weapons later."

The humans exchanged glances. Desmond said, "They could kill us whenever they want, but they haven't. I think we can trust them."

Gideon nodded and handed his gun to Grayface. Terry then handed over his.

Grayface stared at the weapons in his arms with his

perpetually-wide eyes. There was no way to know what the creature was thinking. Finally, he spoke, and Desmond's wrist device translated. "Our young are important to us, and they must be protected and valued. Our young will now come out to meet you. They will perform and entertain you. We think you will enjoy." Grayface then turned and carried the guns away.

Desmond noted that Infinity, Gideon, and the Marines carefully watched the lemur until it disappeared into one of the ground dwellings. Seconds later, Grayface emerged again without the guns and let out a commanding whistle. Abruptly, the feeding lemurs fell silent and hundreds of faces turned skyward.

Desmond looked up. At first he saw only a few dozen tree-houses interspersed among the foliage. Then his eyes were drawn to the largest of the arboreal dwellings, which was suspended above one edge of the clearing, perhaps forty feet from the ground. Lemurs were swarming out of the structure and descending from the tree. These creatures were smaller than the ones on the ground. In fact, some of them appeared to be no more than two feet tall, probably weighing only thirty pounds or so. The largest were perhaps three quarters the size of the adults. By the time the young had all gathered on the ground, Desmond had counted forty-three.

One of the larger children threw its head back and emitted a series of cackles and clicks. Deon was nearest, and his translator responded. "City dwellers say farewell to their families and to their young. They put on their best clothes, and they groom their tails. They give their wealth, hoping to achieve honor. They enter the forest, which they do not enjoy."

About twenty of the older-looking children stepped away from the smaller kids and moved out among the dining adults, walking with exaggerated movements, looking from side to side as if searching.

A noisy ripple spread throughout the crowd, a chittering sound unlike anything Desmond had yet heard from the ringtails. The young creatures then began exaggerating their movements even more, which caused the chittering ripple to grow louder, with some of the adults throwing their heads back and others pointing at specific children as if delighted by the style of their movements. Desmond became convinced the adults were laughing.

As the older kids continued stalking through the crowd, the smaller children began spreading out and moving around the perimeter of the clearing, staying low as if to avoid detection.

Amidst all of this motion, the narrator remained still at the clearing's edge. The kid spoke again, and Deon's translator said, "City dwellers move noisily in the forest. They look for movement. They smell for scent. They do not know they are being watched."

Before Deon's translator had even finished speaking, the crowd's chittering grew even louder. As if on cue, the smaller children around the perimeter began moving into the crowd, still crouching low.

The narrator continued. "The city dwellers cannot find what they are seeking. Their noses can no longer smell because they live in the stink of their city. They make too much noise. They become angry. They become sad."

The audience's chittering laughter began to drown out the speaker on Deon's wrist device. To Desmond's surprise, his own translator, as well as all the others', began speaking simultaneously as one, amplifying the translated words.

"The city dwellers are sad. They have given their wealth,

but they cannot find something to attack and kill. They achieve no honor. They achieve no fun."

The larger kids crouched and feigned anger, slapping the ground, eliciting even more laughter.

Abruptly, the smaller children jumped to their feet, squealing and waving their arms.

The older kids exploded into action, bounding toward their prey, leaping over the heads of some of the seated adults. But just as one of the hunters closed in on its selected target, it tripped and rolled in the dirt, expertly avoiding tumbling into any of the adult spectators. This resulted in a huge surge of roaring laughter.

By this time, all the supposed city dwellers were likewise tripping and falling in overly dramatic and exaggerated ways. As the crowd continued laughing, the city dwellers slowly staggered to their feet and took a fighting stance. Desmond realized they had the same posture he had seen one of the real city dwellers take the previous day just before it had attacked Infinity—fingertips of one hand touching the ground, the other hand clenched into a fist near the face.

The crowd's laughter reached an almost deafening gale.

The smaller children all crouched into the same fighting stance for a moment and then sprung into action, at least twenty children leaping forward and attacking, sending their opponents into absurdly clumsy but well-practiced nosedives and flailing somersaults.

Undaunted, the city dwellers came back for more, only to be pummeled, kicked, or head-butted, again resulting in unflattering antics.

The series of attacks and more-effective counterattacks continued, becoming more farcical and yet more impressive with each round. During all of this, the laughing adults remained untouched, even though the stunts were being acted out only inches away. The youngest lemurs' motions were relatively simple, but the older ones were obviously skilled acrobats. Desmond sat in awe of the performance's choreographic complexity.

Finally, when it seemed the fighting antics couldn't get any more outrageous, the city dwellers all collapsed simultaneously onto the ground one last time and remained still. The smaller lemurs stepped up onto their bodies and let out long, warbling whistles.

The adult lemurs immediately returned the whistles, making so much noise that Desmond had to plug his ears with his fingers. The adults then went back to eating their bug honey.

The kids' performance had apparently been a success.

11

VOLUNTEER

April 11 - 12:11 PM

INFINITY PUSHED the last few globs of food around on the leaf with her finger, wondering if the lemurs would be offended if she didn't finish all of it. Her thoughts then began to swirl in her mind as she tried to make sense of her group's dilemma. Why had Kitty, Tigger, and Teddy selected this particular version of Earth for the trial? Did they intend for the humans to become embroiled in the liberation of these forest-dwelling lemurs? Regardless, the trial's absurd design—judging an entire species and planet based on the actions of a few individuals—was cruel and unfair.

She decided to quit worrying about which actions were right or wrong for now and just focus on keeping the remaining members of her team alive. She had never considered herself all that well suited to matters of ethics anyway.

She swallowed the last bite of her buggy-nectar goo and looked out over the sea of hundreds of seated lemurs. Many of them were stealing not-too-subtle glances in her direction, while others were flat-out staring.

She nudged Desmond. "What do you suppose they're thinking about us?"

He had actually been licking his serving leaf, and he flashed a boyish grin as he quickly put it back on the ground. "I would guess they're fearful and suspicious. They definitely have reason to be, considering all that's been done to them. I mean, humans are certainly guilty of mistreating their fellow humans, but keeping them in enclosures in order to hunt them for sport?" He shook his head.

Gideon, sitting beside them and having apparently overheard, said, "I hunted at a game farm in Texas once. For a price, you could pick the species you wanted to shoot, and they would take you to the right enclosure and guide you within range of one of the animals. Everything but pull the trigger for you."

Infinity raised her brows as she turned back to Desmond.

"Look, I'm not defending human behavior," Desmond said. "But this is different. These lemurs are intelligent—at least as intelligent as we are. All I'm saying is that they have every reason to be fearful and suspicious."

Infinity nodded. "Yeah. Which makes me wonder why they haven't killed us yet."

Bishop, who was sitting across from Infinity, nodded toward something behind her. "Incoming."

She turned. Scarface, Grayface, and another adult male lemur were making their way through the crowd toward the humans. Following them were two juveniles.

The group of lemurs approached the humans and came to a stop. Grayface spoke, and Desmond's wrist device translated. "These children would like to speak to you. Our children are important to us, so you must be respectful, and you must not threaten them or try to harm them. Do you agree?"

Desmond spoke up. "We don't wish to harm anyone. Thank you for introducing us to your children."

The three adult lemurs listened to the translation and then stepped aside. The juveniles moved forward, their round eyes flitting back and forth between the humans. Infinity noticed that both were females, each with two pairs of diminutive nipples on her abdomen. The nearest girl was slightly taller, but other than that the two appeared to be identical.

One of them spoke, her cackles and clicks noticeably higher in pitch than the adults. When she was finished, Desmond's translator said, "I have not seen animals like you. You look strange, and your talking makes me want to laugh."

Desmond shot Infinity a smile and then replied. "Yes, I understand why we would look and sound funny to you. We come from a different place, where people like us are the only creatures that can talk."

The two juveniles cocked their heads as they listened to the translation. They chittered loudly, apparently laughing. Then the shorter girl spoke. "Your talking is funny, and the things you say are funny. You don't have tails. That is very funny. What happened to your tails?" As Desmond was considering how to respond, the young lemurs flicked their black and white tails as if flaunting them.

He turned, displaying his backside. "Our species doesn't have tails. But there are animals where we came from that have tails. In fact, most of them have tails. I must say, your tails are... nice."

The girls listened to the translation and chittered again. They turned to each other, extended both hands, and did some kind of rapid gesture in which their fingertips touched.

It reminded Infinity of a fist bump. The taller girl then spoke. "Why did the city dwellers put you in our enclosure?"

Desmond glanced at Infinity again, this time frowning.

Infinity decided to answer the question. "The city dwellers don't know we are here in your enclosure. They attacked us, and we ran away. We came here on our own."

Desmond quickly added, "And we are happy to meet you."

The girls chattered together for a moment, and Desmond's translator didn't respond. The taller girl then turned back to Desmond. "We are happy to meet you, too. We will be sad when the city dwellers kill you. We hope you will fight them with honor. But you don't look like fighters. They will kill you easily. But I will be sad when they kill you."

Before the translator even finished speaking, Grayface barked at the girl, apparently scolding her. She blinked her massive eyes at him and let out a few soft whistles.

Infinity spoke to the girl. "What makes you think they will kill us? They didn't see us come into your enclosure. They don't even know we're here."

The girl looked at Infinity and blinked again. She spoke, and Infinity's translator responded. "Were you hunted where you came from, or did you hunt others?"

Infinity cursed silently. Grayface had apparently told the girl to change the subject. "The place we came from originally was home to only one intelligent species—only one kind of animal that could talk, and we did not hunt each other. But we had to leave that world. Some of us," she pointed to Desmond and Gideon, "moved to a place that was home for one other intelligent species. But we were friends with them, and we did not hunt each other."

After listening to the translation, the two girls chattered to each other for a moment, and then the smaller one spoke to Infinity. "I think your words are funny. You tell funny stories."

Infinity waited for her translator to continue, but it remained silent. Apparently this was all the girl wanted to say.

The taller girl spoke up again, beginning with chittering laughter and then launching into an extended sequence of whistles, squeals, and purrs. Infinity's translator began responding while the girl was still speaking. "My father told funny stories sometimes. He was killed on his first hunt. I was sad then. But he was happy to take his turn in the hunt. My mother was killed on her fourth hunt. She killed three city dwellers before a city dweller killed her, and I was not sad. She fought with honor, and she gave life to three others who would have taken their turns if she had died on her first hunt."

Infinity's translator paused, perhaps struggling to process the lengthy stream of language. The young lemur continued talking, and after several seconds the device resumed. "I will now tell you how I will fight in my first hunt. I have been learning this for many days. I will climb into a long-pod tree, and I will pretend I am busy eating the white flowers. I will let the city dweller see me. The city dweller will think I am not aware, and the city dweller will approach the tree, thinking it will be easy to leap up and pull me to the ground and kill me with its hands and feet."

The translator paused again for a few seconds. "But I will have something the city dweller will not know about." The girl reached out and accepted an object handed to her by the third adult standing with Scarface and Grayface. The girl held the object up, gripped in her long fingers. It was green, about ten inches long, and the tip was pointed. The object looked very much like a seedpod from a catalpa tree. "I made this," the girl said, although she had already lowered the pod back to her side by the time the words came from the translator. "It is not a real long-pod—it just looks like one. Now I will show you how I will kill my first city dweller."

The girl lunged toward Scarface and leapt onto her shoulders. Infinity tensed up, unsure what was happening. The girl continued chattering. "I will be low in the long-pod tree. The stupid city dweller will pull me to the ground."

The smaller girl suddenly jumped up, grabbed the first girl's wrist, and pulled her down from her perch. The girl narrating the story tumbled and hit the ground, landing on her back with a thud. The smaller girl became a blur of motion, putting her friend in a kind of scissor chokehold, with her legs around the narrator's neck and her arms locked around the taller girl's legs to immobilize them.

The narrator continued speaking, although with some difficulty. "The city dweller will try to kill me like this, because this is a city dweller's favorite killing maneuver. But remember, I will have my weapon." She held out her home-made seedpod weapon and hesitated, waiting until Infinity's translator had finished speaking. She then flicked the weapon inward toward her own groin, appearing to plunge it into the younger girl's neck.

The young girl sputtered and rolled away, gripping her throat. The narrator smoothly jumped to her feet and jabbed the pod into the smaller girl's neck again and again. Infinity had to look closely to reassure herself that the stabs were not real but rather convincingly simulated. The younger girl's gruesome gargling noises quickly gave way to chittering laughter. She was apparently delighted to have played a role in the demonstration.

The taller girl finally halted her thrusts and stood up straight, facing the humans. "This is how I will kill in my first hunt. The city dweller will not get a yellow band on that day. I have not decided yet how I will kill my second city dweller, but I will. And I will kill a third. Maybe I will even kill a fourth, and then no city dweller will ever get a yellow band for killing me. I will go on my hunts with honor, and I will give life to others who will not have to take their turns."

The smaller girl finally stopped chittering and rose to her feet. She said, "My mother and father were killed on their first hunts. But I will not be killed. I will learn to fight, and when it is my turn, I will not be afraid."

Infinity stared at the two girls for several seconds, waiting for Desmond to say something reasonable. But he remained silent, and so did Gideon and the Marines. These lemurs, who were at least as intelligent as humans, lived in a world in which they had to train their children to find dignity in being slaughtered. Infinity's own childhood hadn't been all candy and teddy bears, but she had no idea what it would be like to grow up knowing she'd eventually be hunted down and killed for sport. What could she or any other human possibly say to these kids?

She sighed and turned to the taller girl. "You're missing a good opportunity to weaken your attacker before they take you to the ground." She waited for her device to translate and then proceeded. "The city dwellers are larger than you, and they are skilled at grappling on the ground. You have a good plan, but you need to wound your attacker *before* you hit the ground."

Again she waited on the translation and then instructed the girl to take her previous position on Scarface's shoulders. Once the girl was in position, Infinity reached up and gripped her elbow. "The city dweller will expect you to flail helplessly as you fall. This gives you an opportunity to surprise him—or her." She pushed the girl up into a standing position on Scarface's shoulders. "If you position yourself vertically in the tree, your attacker will have to grab your leg instead of your arm. He'll probably grab your nearest leg, so have your weapon ready in your opposite hand. When the city dweller pulls you from the tree, turn your body at the waist and thrust your weapon into his eye. If you aim well and strike hard enough, it will go all the way into his brain and kill him. At the very least, it will slow him down, giving you an advantage when you grapple with him on the ground."

Infinity waited to make sure the girl understood what she had said, and then she began guiding her through the motions. "Practice this move until you can do it with your eyes closed. And be sure to practice it with the weapon in your other hand too—the city dweller could attack from either side."

The girl chittered with apparent delight. "Yes, I will kill my first city dweller this way. I like your funny talking. I will be sad when a city dweller kills you."

Grayface barked at the girl again, and she promptly leapt off Scarface's shoulders and positioned herself beside the younger girl. Grayface barked once more, and the two girls scampered away, laughing together as they ran.

Grayface turned to the humans. "You were respectful to our children, as we requested. We will return your weapons now." The lemur barked a few orders, and soon a male lemur brought out the two dart guns and handed them over to Gideon and Terry.

Grayface spoke again. "Soon you must leave our home and our enclosure. We do not want the city dwellers to come to our home looking for you. We hope that you are learning from us. We hope that you are learning how you can be happy even when the city dwellers hunt and kill one of you every day, because that surely will be your future."

As if prompted by some silent signal, the hundreds of lemurs surrounding the humans all began getting to their feet.

Most of the chattering stopped, and a somber silence settled in as the crowd began shuffling toward one end of the clearing.

Grayface watched some of the lemurs walking past and then spoke to the humans. "Now is the time for the daily hunt. You should observe our procedures—our rituals. Our rituals help us to be happy. You can learn to be happy. Follow me."

Grayface waited for the translation to end and then gestured for the humans to follow him. He then led them away with the rest of the crowd.

At the edge of the treehouse village, the lemurs and humans gathered in silence around a single adult male who was intensely focused on grooming his black and white tail.

Once the entire group was in position, an adult female Infinity didn't recognize began talking to the lemur who was grooming his tail. The female appeared to be even older than Scarface and Grayface, and she had more scars on her face and body than either of them. Infinity decided to call her Scarbody.

Grayface, apparently recognizing that the translators weren't responding, turned to the humans and spoke directly to them. Infinity's translator interpreted. "The individual you see before you is preparing for the hunt. His turn is today. We have rituals for choosing turns. We choose turns many days ahead. We choose turns by many factors, including age and length of time since the individual's last turn. Also, individuals may volunteer for turns. To volunteer for a turn is honorable, because it gives life to another who would otherwise have a turn on that day. To injure or to kill a hunting city dweller is also honorable, because it allows the victor to have another turn, which also gives life to another. If an individual kills hunting city dwellers on four hunts, they never have to take another turn. There are only three among us who never have to take another turn." Grayface waited for the translator to finish and then pointed to his own forehead. He then pointed to Scarface, and finally to Scarbody.

Everyone turned their attention back to the lemur at the center of the gathering, who had finally finished grooming his tail and was now standing stone-still, staring at Scarbody, who was still speaking to him.

"We are asking if he would like to give his turn to another," Grayface said to the humans. "He has three children, and the children's mother did not return from her only hunt. Therefore, giving his turn to another would bring him little dishonor. However, he is now indicating that he does not wish to do so."

Infinity said, "What would happen if *no one* went to the hunt? What if you all just stayed here?"

Grayface responded. "The city dweller would become angry and would come to our home and attack the first individual it encountered. This would not be fair, because it would not be that individual's turn."

One of the Marines, Terry, spoke up. "What if two of you go on the hunt? Or three? Hell, ten of you could go, and you could kill the hunter with ease."

Grayface blinked several times as he listened to the translation. "We have tried many strategies—more strategies than I could describe without becoming tired of describing. The hunter is accompanied always by other city dwellers who document the hunt. They document the hunt with devices that make pictures—cameras. If two or more of us go on the hunt, or if we violate the rules in any other way, the city dwellers will know. Then the city dwellers will come to our home with vehicles and weapons. They will destroy our home, and we will have to rebuild. They will cause hardship for us, and still they will hunt one of us each day. They will hunt one of us each day, always. We have learned to be happy anyway. You can learn to be happy, too."

Infinity listened to the lengthy translation and then glanced at each of her human companions in turn. They were all staring grimly at the lemur in the center of the crowd, who was still standing motionless. Scarbody finally stopped speaking to the lemur, stepped forward, and handed the creature a polished stick about three feet long.

The lemur accepted the stick, and Scarbody stepped back. The lemur then crouched abruptly into a fighting stance, the fingers of his right hand touching the ground and his left hand gripping the stick beside his left cheek. The crowd erupted into a chorus of enthusiastic whistles and chirps.

Grayface spoke to the humans again. "The city dwellers allow us to defend ourselves with weapons, but the weapons must be small and simple. The city dwellers never use weapons when they hunt us, because they achieve more honor by killing us without using weapons. A city dweller gets a yellow band when they kill one of us. Then they wear the yellow band on their leg. This brings them honor. If they kill us when we are using a weapon, they get a yellow band with blue markings. This brings them even more honor."

The lemur held his stance for some seconds and then launched abruptly into a series of fighting moves. Infinity stared in awe as the creature's moves became faster and more elaborate. In an intricately-choreographed dance, the stick spun and sliced through the air audibly, loud enough to be heard even over the appreciative vocalizations of the crowd. Infinity was skeptical about how well the moves in this performance would serve the lemur in an actual fight to the death, but the whole thing was still breathtaking to watch.

After at least a full minute of all-out exertion, the lemur finally stopped. Gripping his stick in one hand, he headed for the forest, and the crowd parted to allow him through. The lemurs stared after him in complete silence until he was no longer visible.

Grayface turned and spoke to Infinity's group again. "He will go to the place where city dwellers always come to hunt us. The city dwellers believe that their skill allows them to find us, but in reality we always go to them. The city dwellers are skilled fighters, but they are not skilled hunters."

Infinity shook her head solemnly. The ring-tail was offering himself up, knowing he would most likely be killed.

Infinity glanced around, expecting the crowd to begin dispersing, but everyone remained still and silent. Several minutes passed, and still the lemurs scarcely moved a muscle. She sensed that they were waiting for something to happen, but there was nothing to see but dense forest.

"What the hell are we doing?" asked Deon.

Several of the lemurs shot looks at the Marine, but their stoic faces and wide eyes revealed no meaning. The creatures quickly went back to watching the forest.

Infinity pressed her finger to her lips and made sure each of the other humans saw the gesture.

More time passed, at least another fifteen minutes.

Some of the lemurs had begun shifting back and forth, apparently agitated. Several whimpers and soft whistles arose from individuals in the group but were quickly silenced by stares from the others.

Then, a long, warbling cry filtered through the trees from a distance, the same victory cry the children had used in their performance. The crowd responded almost immediately, filling the air with the same warbling cry. Some of the ring-tails turned to each other and exchanged the rapid, finger-touching gesture Infinity had seen earlier between the two juvenile girls. There was no mistaking the elated mood of the crowd.

As the lemurs celebrated, Infinity watched the forest, expecting the hunted lemur to return victorious. But several minutes passed with no sign of him, and the crowd's enthusiasm began to fade.

One of the lemurs barked and pointed into the trees. Infinity looked. She saw movement—something approaching. It was the male lemur returning, but one side of his body was covered in blood, and his left arm was dangling loosely from his shoulder. He stumbled and fell, and the crowd surged forward to provide assistance.

Infinity, caught up in the excitement, ran with them, followed by Desmond and the others.

By the time she made her way over, hundreds of ring-tails had already gathered around the injured lemur, and she was only able to catch glimpses of what was happening.

"Can you see anything?" Gideon asked as he and others came to a stop beside her. "Is he okay?"

Infinity shook her head. "No idea." She moved around the crowd but still couldn't see.

The mass of lemurs began moving back toward the village. Infinity glimpsed some of them carrying their injured companion. But then something else caught her eye, and she turned to look. It was another creature, larger than the forest-dwelling ring-tails and with a longer tail of solid brown rather than black and white. It was a city-dwelling lemur. The creature was walking toward Infinity, aiming something dark directly at her.

She instinctively dropped to the ground, assuming the creature was about to shoot her. The lemur kept coming.

"That must be one of the documenters of the hunt," Desmond said loudly. "With a camera."

"Dammit!" Gideon said. "He's already seen us."

Infinity saw Terry raise his weapon out of the corner of her eye. Before she could shout for him to stop, she heard a sharp snap as he fired, followed two seconds later by another snap as he fired again.

The lemur dropped the camera and collapsed onto its back.

"Well," said Terry, "he ain't taking that camera back to the city."

Infinity jumped to her feet and yanked the gun from Terry's hands. "What do you think you're doing?"

The Marine scowled at her, but then his features softened, and he shot an uncertain glance at the dead city dweller. "I figured it was a good use of my last two rounds."

Grayface stepped between Infinity and Terry, his gaze fixed on the fallen lemur. He barked and growled loudly. Infinity's translator said, "You must leave this place now. Go quickly."

"They won't know we're here," Terry said, his voice cracking. "We can just hide the body. They'll assume he got lost or something."

Grayface turned to Terry. "The camera sends images to the city dwellers during the hunt. It is sending images now. The city dwellers already know you are here."

Terry's face went pale. "Shit."

Desmond grabbed Grayface's elbow. "We're so sorry. What will the city dwellers do to you and your village?"

Grayface replied, "Nothing they haven't done many times before. You must go now. Go quickly."

Infinity heard something and snapped her head to the side. It was a chittering, mechanical sound, and it was getting louder with every passing second.

12

———

PURSUIT

DESMOND TRIPPED on something and face-planted in the mud and dead leaves. Pain shot through his face, and he scrambled back to his feet.

Infinity had come to a stop and was looking back at him with a frown.

"It's these pants," he muttered as he began picking up speed again. "They aren't well designed for running."

"Just keep quiet," she hissed. "We have no idea what tech they're using to track us."

They ran in silence for about a hundred yards until they reached Gideon and the Marines, who had paused to wait for them. The humans formed a tight circle and stood gasping for air.

"I'm sorry, guys," Terry whispered. "I had no idea the camera had a live feed."

Infinity shook her head, turned away, and gazed back into

the forest. Gideon and the other Marines eyed Terry impassively, showing neither contempt nor support.

Desmond felt sorry for Terry. The guy couldn't have been much older than twenty. "The outcome wouldn't have been any different if you hadn't shot the creature," Desmond said. "They'd still know we're here, and we'd still be running for our lives."

Terry nodded slightly but still looked distressed.

"I still hear them," Gideon said, his head cocked. "Getting closer. They must be tracking us somehow."

Desmond listened. Gideon was right—the chittering vehicles were catching up. The humans had run at least a mile through dense forest, and Desmond now felt completely lost. Grayface had said the city dwellers themselves were poor hunters, but maybe their vehicles could track by thermal signatures or even scents.

"Well, we can't keep running," Infinity said.

"We could climb the trees," Gideon suggested.

Infinity shook her head. "Been treed too many times. Doesn't end well. Maybe a river or stream. Might lose them walking the stream bed or swimming."

Desmond nodded. "Okay, let's keep going until we find one. If the terrain starts to slope, we head downhill." Unfortunately, the ground they'd covered so far had been utterly flat, and there was no reason to think any particular direction would be different.

Infinity didn't waste any more time discussing it—she nodded once and took off again. Desmond and the others followed.

They ran for another quarter mile or so until they were stopped by a fence. The mesh was similar to that of the enclosure fence they'd climbed through yesterday, and this fence was just as tall. But the top was different, curved outward on both sides, apparently designed to stop climbers coming from either direction. The fence extended through the forest as far as Desmond could see in either direction.

Vic put his hand on the mesh and pushed, testing its strength. "Must be the border of the ring-tails' enclosure."

"Could be just what we need to slow them down," Infinity said. She started jogging to the left alongside the fence. "This way. Look for an opening."

As Desmond started after her, he could already hear the vehicles catching up again.

It didn't take long to find a gap between the fence's bottom edge and the ground. Although the fence had probably been an impressive barrier originally, the city dwellers obviously hadn't maintained it.

As the humans crawled under the fence one at a time, Desmond tried not to dwell on the fact that they were now trespassing into the territory of another species that might be far less friendly than the ring-tails.

Desmond was the last one through, and the others had already taken off running by the time Infinity pulled him to his feet. The city dwellers' vehicles now sounded so close that he expected them to come into view at any moment. Infinity whispered something he couldn't make out and then took off after the others.

As Desmond ran to catch up, he glanced back and saw them—three multi-legged vehicles, each with two black-clad riders sitting side-by-side. One of the vehicles was already at the fence, and several of its appendages were snapping back and forth in a blur. It was cutting its way through.

"It's no use!" he cried to Infinity. "They're coming through the fence."

She glanced back and then turned to the others, who were about forty yards ahead. "Gideon! We have to split up."

Gideon turned and looked back. He said something to the four Marines, and they cut to the left while Gideon cut to the right. He then beckoned to Desmond and Infinity. "Come on!"

They angled to the right, following him.

Desmond looked back again. It was too late. The city dwellers had spotted them, and now one of the vehicles was barreling straight at them, its mechanical feet flinging leaves and dirt into the air.

By the time Desmond and Infinity had caught up with Gideon, the machine was nearly upon them.

The riders, or perhaps the vehicle itself, barked and whistled, activating Desmond's translator. "Stop. Stop now."

Infinity kept running and shot Desmond a look. "They're too fast. Get behind a tree and keep it between you and them." She skidded to a stop and ducked behind a thick trunk.

Desmond joined her behind the same tree. He peeked around the edge just in time to see the vehicle come to an abrupt stop not ten feet away. The two lemurs dismounted immediately, split up, and circled around the tree on either side. They both took up positions about five feet from Desmond and Infinity, crouching into the now-familiar fighting stance, with the fingers of one hand pressed against the ground. Desmond's eyes were drawn to their legs. Their feet were bare, but their ankles were adorned with bands of various colors. One of the two wore a band of yellow with distinct blue markings.

The lemur with the yellow band chattered rapidly, and Infinity's translator said, "Do not fight. If you fight, we kill."

Desmond sensed Infinity tensing up to attack, and he put a hand on her arm. He spoke to the city dwellers. "We don't want to fight, and we don't want trouble. We just want to be left alone. Please, just let us go."

The device on his wrist began translating, and the lemurs briefly flicked their eyes from his face to the translator as it converted his words into what he hoped was an accurate translation.

The now-riderless vehicle stepped into view. It turned and pointed its front end directly at Desmond and Infinity. Desmond wondered how many weapons it was pointing at them.

The same lemur spoke again. "You come with us now."

An angry shout—distinctly human—came from the direction of the Marines, followed by frantic cursing. It sounded like they were under attack.

"Goddammit!" Infinity growled. She launched herself at the nearest lemur and slammed a fist down onto the creature's head. She then rolled on the ground with the lemur until the tree was between her and the vehicle. In the process, she somehow managed to get the lemur into a headlock and yank it around until its abdomen was facing Desmond.

Her eyes met Desmond's. "Now!"

He dropped to his knees to ram his fist into the lemur's throat, but then he heard a loud pop and felt something hit his side. The stuff was wet and sticky, and his arms were entangled in it. He tried to strike the immobilized lemur, but the substance tightened its grip every time he moved. In his peripheral vision he saw the second lemur rushing at him. The creature jump-kicked him in the shoulder, and he tumbled onto his side.

He struggled even harder to free his arms, but it was no use. He watched helplessly as the lemur who had kicked him stepped casually over to Infinity and stared down at her and her struggling captive.

She glared up at the creature and tightened her grip,

grunting from the effort, threatening to break the lemur's neck.

The standing lemur barked at her, and her translator said, "Release now."

"Do what it says, Infinity," Desmond sputtered. "They'll kill you."

She continued glaring up at the lemur for several more seconds, her lip twitching, but then she relaxed her arms. Her captive rolled away and leapt to its feet.

A split-second later, another pop came from the robot vehicle, and a yellow, softball-sized blob slammed into Infinity's body. The blob splattered, and stringy goo ensnared her arms. She struggled to free herself, but as Desmond had already discovered, the tiniest threads of the stuff were too strong to break, and they became tighter by the second. Infinity was completely immobilized.

The lemur she had released crouched with both hands on the ground and stared into her eyes. The creature cooed and whistled softly at her. Her translator said, "You are a fighter. We are glad you are a fighter." The lemur continued looking at her, apparently waiting for a response.

Suddenly the creature flopped onto its back, blood spewing from an opening in the side of its head. The other lemur screeched and spun around, looking about frantically.

This time, Desmond heard the snap of a dart weapon. The second lemur's legs began spasming before it even hit the ground. The creature landed with a thud and began floundering, its legs trembling against the dead leaves on the forest floor so rapidly that the sound reminded Desmond of a rattlesnake.

"You two okay?"

Desmond twisted around until he saw Gideon peering cautiously from behind a tree.

The lemurs' vehicle shifted position abruptly to face Gideon.

A pop came from the robot, and a portion of the tree near Gideon's head exploded.

"Shit!" he cried as he pulled back behind the tree.

The robot took a few steps forward and fired again, blasting more bark and wood from the tree. It moved another five feet closer and shot again, leaving a massive crater in the trunk.

"I have nine darts left," Gideon called out. "What's that damn robot made of?"

Desmond frowned at Infinity. He then looked at the vehicle. "Not sure. Looks like some kind of plastic. You're not going to try to—"

"Yes he is!" Infinity proclaimed. With her arms still stuck to her torso, she struggled to her knees and then to her feet. "Gideon, on my mark!" Before Desmond realized what she was doing, she charged the vehicle from behind and slid into it, kicking two of its three left legs out from under it. "Okay, now!" she cried as the massive machine staggered and almost fell on top of her.

Desmond saw Gideon stepping out from behind the tree but didn't wait to see what would happen next. He got to his feet and started running toward the vehicle. Infinity was on her back, kicking at its legs. Desmond slid in beside her and slammed into two of its right legs, causing it to stagger again.

Desmond heard a *thunk*, and then two more, as Gideon's projectiles struck the robot. Desmond and Infinity continued frantically kicking the vehicle's legs, trying to keep it from regaining its stability.

Another *thunk*, and then another.

The vehicle collapsed onto its side. One of its flailing legs struck Desmond's shin, sending pain shooting up his leg, and another almost caught him in the face as he and Infinity rolled out of the machine's reach.

Lemur vocalizations came from a speaker somewhere on the struggling vehicle. Desmond's translator said, "You must not damage me. If you damage me, I will kill."

Thunk, thunk. Two more projectiles pelted the robot's body as Gideon fired at it from only a few feet away.

The vehicle fell silent. Four of its six legs became still. The last two were still moving pitifully, as if trying to walk in slow motion.

Desmond stared up at Gideon. "I'd forgotten how crazy you are, man."

Gideon half-smiled. "Only when I need to be." He lifted his weapon and eyed the magazine. "Only two darts left."

Infinity was struggling to free herself. "A little help here?"

Gideon kneeled beside her and pulled at one of the sinewy strands of yellow goo. He pulled harder but couldn't get it to break. "Hold on," he said. He stepped over to the damaged vehicle, grabbed one of its legs, and inspected the clawed foot. "This looks sharp enough." He stepped back over to Infinity and looked down at her with his mouth twisted, like he wasn't sure how to move her. "Sorry about this," he said. Then he grabbed her collar, dragged her over to the mechanical leg, and began using the claw to cut away the strands binding her arms.

A few minutes later, most of the severed strands lay in a heap on the ground. Gideon then dragged Desmond into Infinity's place for his turn.

Infinity got to her feet and began picking off the remaining severed bits. "I don't hear anything. If the other city dwellers had killed the Marines, they'd have come after us by now."

Desmond got to one knee, rubbing his shin where the

vehicle had kicked him—it was definitely sore but didn't seem to be broken. "Maybe the guys got away and the lemurs are still tracking them."

Gideon shook his head. "More likely the lemurs caught them and are now occupied with managing prisoners."

"Gideon's right," Infinity said. "Here's the way I see it. We can run and hide, maybe survive a few more hours. Or we can help the rest of our team. We'll probably get killed in the process. But we have to assume Kitty is still watching us, judging us. Maybe our actions will convince her we're a worthy species." She tapped her forehead where the camera was embedded. "You hear that, Kitty? If that's not enough for you, then you and the rest of your fuzzy-ass kind can go to hell."

Desmond frowned at her. "I don't think antagonizing Kitty could possibly—"

"I don't care! I've had it with this goddamn trial." She turned and started walking in the direction they had last seen the Marines. "We're wasting time. We need to get to the Marines before this place is crawling with more city dwellers."

Desmond and Gideon exchanged glances and then followed.

"Hey," Desmond said as he caught up to Infinity. "You okay?"

She slid her hand into his and squeezed. "Exhausted. And really pissed. We shouldn't even be here."

"At least we're here together."

She glanced at him, and one edge of her mouth turned up slightly. "For the moment. We could be dead ten minutes from now. Just in case, you know how I feel, right?"

He studied the side of her face. Underneath all the blood and grime, he could see several old scars, some of which she'd gotten before he met her. She was the only person he'd ever truly fallen in love with. And he knew she loved him, although she wasn't much for actually saying the words. He formed a vision of the two of them lying on a beach in front of a red, setting sun and projected the image through his arm, into her hand, and up to her mind. He then spoke aloud. "Yeah, I do know," he said, "and you know I feel the same."

Gideon was walking behind them, and he responded to the audible portion of their exchange with a grunt.

A loud sequence of lemur vocalizations sounded several hundred yards ahead. Desmond paused to listen. "It's coming from the speakers on one of the vehicles."

"They must be talking to the Marines," Gideon said. "That means at least one of them must still be alive. Maybe we should split up—come at them from different directions."

Infinity shrugged. "It's hard to say without knowing the situation. Let's see if we can get close enough to make an assessment first."

They crept forward, trying to avoid stepping on sticks and dry leaves.

Soon Desmond spotted one of the vehicles. Only one rider was sitting on it.

The three humans circled around quietly until they could approach from behind a clump of trees.

Desmond spotted the other vehicle, this one with both riders. The two vehicles were facing each other, perhaps twenty yards apart. They appeared to be confronting something between them, but that space was obscured by trees and brush.

"Why are they just sitting there?" Gideon whispered.

Infinity ignored the question and gestured for them to move closer.

They inched their way forward and to the right until they could see the space between the two vehicles. Desmond blinked and shifted his head from side to side to make sure the remaining brush wasn't distorting his vision. But there was no mistaking it. The four Marines were there, two of them lying on the ground motionless, the other two on their knees. Surrounding the Marines were at least fifteen lemurs.

But these lemurs were neither city dwellers nor ring-tails. They appeared to be another species entirely. The creatures were similar in size to the ring-tails—weighing perhaps a hundred pounds each—but they were almost entirely white except for their black faces and bronze arms. Even their legs and their fluffy tails were solid white. Like the ring-tails, these white lemurs wore no clothing. They were all facing outward, apparently protecting the huddled Marines from the city dwellers.

Desmond looked around for the fourth city dweller and spotted it lying motionless about thirty yards behind the vehicle that was missing a rider. Somehow the Marines—or maybe the white lemurs—had managed to incapacitate one of the attackers.

"Looks like a standoff," Gideon whispered.

Desmond nodded. "Yeah, and it looks like we may have some new allies."

One of the vehicles emitted another stream of amplified lemur vocalizations. Desmond was tempted to ask his wrist device to translate, but although the device was impressive, he doubted it was smart enough to keep its volume low.

"They seem to be reluctant to shoot the white lemurs," Infinity whispered. "I'm betting because wealthy city dwellers will pay big bucks to hunt them." She turned and looked at Gideon and then at Desmond, her jaw muscles tightened with resolve. "The only advantage we have is the element of surprise. So I say we surprise the hell out of them." She glanced at Gideon's gun. "You said you have two more darts?"

He nodded.

"Do you think you can get close enough to take out the single rider?"

He turned toward the vehicle, his eyes scanning the groundcover to the left and right of it. "Good chance I could. This thing's wicked accurate."

Infinity's jaw muscles rippled as she thought for a moment. "Then this is what I think we should do," she finally said. "It may not work, but it's the best plan I've got. At the very least, hopefully it'll show Kitty how determined we are to take care of our own."

Desmond's gut began to knot up. Infinity wouldn't bother to explain all this unless she really believed there was a good chance the plan would fail.

She gazed intensely at Desmond. "The moment Gideon shoots the single rider, I'm going to take out the pair of riders on the other vehicle. At that same moment, you're going to jump on the first vehicle and make it attack the other one."

Desmond stared back at her. "You're not serious! I have no idea how to control that thing. It was created by an entirely different species."

"You're a hell of a lot smarter than I am. You're going to have to figure it out."

"In ten seconds? Because that's how much time I'll have before the vehicle starts shooting at you."

Her stare didn't waiver. "Maybe you can use that thought projection thing you do." She put a hand on his arm. "Please, Desmond, you have to do this. We're not letting those bastards take the Marines without a fight."

He started to open his mouth to object again, but then he just shook his head in bewilderment.

Infinity's eyes flicked to Gideon. "You in?"

Gideon rubbed his forehead as if he had a migraine. But then he nodded grimly. "Give me two minutes to get in place."

"You got it" she said. "By that time, I should be in position too. Desmond, follow Gideon and get yourself near enough to take that robot when the rider drops." Her eyes lingered on him briefly, just long enough to make him want to reach out and embrace her in case he never had the opportunity again. But then it was too late—she crouched and began making her way quietly around to the other side of the circle of lemurs.

Gideon cuffed Desmond's back gently with his palm. "She's right, you know. If we're going to die anyway, we might as well do a bang-up job of it. Maybe earn a few points."

Desmond tried to steady his breathing. "I doubt suicide is the only way to earn points, but it looks like I'm outvoted. I'll do my best." He paused. "You know we both think of you as family, don't you?"

Gideon nodded once. "Damn right." He then ducked and started creeping toward the single rider.

As Desmond followed, one of the robots spoke again. One of the white lemurs answered with rapid vocalizations, but Desmond's translator again remained silent, and he was grateful that it only worked when someone was speaking directly to him.

He and Gideon moved silently, using any available brush as cover. When they were about thirty yards out, Gideon turned to Desmond and nodded, signaling that this was close enough. Desmond crept forward another few yards. At least two minutes had now passed, if not more. He looked back at Gideon and nodded. The guardsman carefully raised his weapon and looked down the sights. He then took a deep breath and held it. Desmond turned his attention back to the robot rider. His pulse was pounding in his ears, and he had to fight the impulse to spring into action before Gideon took the shot.

Several long seconds passed.

Gideon's gun fired with a snap.

Desmond didn't wait to see if the shot was good—he leapt up and used every bit of speed he could muster to close the distance to the vehicle. His feet pounding the ground, he glimpsed a figure tumbling off the vehicle toward him. He jumped between two of the robot's legs, soared over the falling figure, and slammed into the chassis. Grabbing at whatever he could, he swung a leg over the vehicle.

The machine was now turning beneath him, perhaps confused. Lemur vocalizations and human shouts came from somewhere, but Desmond didn't dare take his eyes off the mechanical beast beneath him. His hands found protrusions to grip, and he pushed himself upright to look at the vehicle's controls.

He saw nothing that even remotely resembled buttons, levers, or any other mechanical controls. How the hell did the city dwellers drive these things?

The robot kept turning, first one direction then the other.

"Desmond!" It was Infinity's voice, and she was screaming at him, but he couldn't even tell the direction.

There was a pop, and then another—the unmistakable sound of shots fired by one of the vehicle's weapons.

He cried out, "Infinity! I... can't do anything!" The robot suddenly bucked violently, maybe because it had heard his voice, and he was nearly thrown from the vehicle.

He was now holding on with only one hand. Had Infinity been shot? He didn't dare take his attention off the vehicle. He started frantically punching and pulling everything he could find with his free hand, hoping to get lucky and discover a control. Nothing was working. It was hopeless, and it was too late.

The vehicle's movements were becoming even more erratic. Desmond threw his chest against the machine and held on with both hands. He was starting to panic, not seeing any way out of the situation. Then he remembered Infinity saying something. Projecting his thoughts—that was it. It probably wouldn't work, but he had no other options. At any moment the vehicle might flip itself over and crush him to death.

He pressed his chest and cheek against the machine's shell and formed words in his mind. "Stop turning and attack the other vehicle. Do it now!"

Nothing. The thing just kept turning.

He grunted in frustration. Now what? Then something occurred to him. Of course the machine couldn't understand his words—he was speaking English. He tried again, this time forming a mental vision of the vehicle charging the other one, knocking it over, and kicking the crap out of it. He imagined the vision traveling from his head, into his arms, and into the vehicle's mind—or processor, or whatever.

The vehicle stopped.

Inches from Desmond's head, a series of deafening pops came from the machine, at least ten in a row. The vehicle then fell silent beneath him and remained still.

"Holy crap!" someone said.

Desmond situated himself on the robot's back and righted himself into a sitting position. About twenty yards away, the other vehicle lay mangled and motionless. It wasn't even twitching. To one side was Infinity, sitting on her butt and staring at Desmond with an expression that could almost have passed for a smile. The two city dwellers from the other vehicle were sprawled on the ground, both of them alive and being held down by white lemurs. Two other white lemurs were lying motionless and bloody.

Gideon walked up from behind Desmond, his weapon resting on one shoulder. "Well, what now? The plan wasn't supposed to actually work."

One of the white lemurs pointed at Desmond and emitted a few barks and whistles. Desmond's translator said, "Confusion. Questions. Who?"

Apparently these lemurs didn't speak the same language as the ring-tails or the city dwellers.

The lemur that had spoken turned and stared toward the enclosure fence, apparently listening. Then the others did the same. One of them squealed, and the entire group erupted into chaotic chattering.

Desmond's eyes met Infinity's. She said something, but he couldn't hear her over the lemurs' cacophony. Most likely she was pointing out that more city dwellers were probably coming, and it was time to go.

He glanced at the Marines. Two of them, Deon and Bishop, were unconscious or dead. The other two, Vic and Terry, would no doubt be reluctant to leave them behind.

Desmond tightened his grip on the machine beneath him and projected a vision of the robot walking over and stopping beside the Marines. The robot responded.

The chattering lemurs immediately fell silent and backed up a few steps. A couple of them pointed into the forest, presumably in the direction of more approaching city dwellers. Desmond didn't break his concentration to look—it was already obvious there was no time to waste.

"Terry, Vic," said Desmond, pointing to the two motionless Marines. "Put them on the vehicle. We have to go."

"No point," Terry said. "They're already dead."

Vic added, "We'd be dead, too, if it weren't for our new friends here."

Some of the white lemurs were starting to move away into the forest, and Desmond got the feeling that the whole group was about to break and run. Several of the white lemurs were still restraining two of the city dwellers. He projected a vision of his vehicle stepping over to the restrained city dwellers and pressing a leg against each of them to hold them down. If the vehicle would actually comply, he could jump off and flee with Infinity and the others.

As his robot responded to his command, he heard the chittering of more vehicles approaching. They were close—really close. His machine began walking toward the restrained city dwellers but then stopped several feet short. He projected the vision again. The robot began to take another step but stopped again. It wouldn't comply.

Most of the white lemurs had already begun fleeing, disappearing into the forest. Finally, those holding the city dwellers down released their prisoners and fled, running on all fours, their tails bouncing above their backs.

Infinity and Vic charged the two city dwellers to keep them from getting up, but the creatures had already lifted themselves to a fighting stance and were ready. The four tumbled into a mess of thrashing arms and legs. Desmond leapt off his now-useless robot as Gideon and Terry rushed to join the fray. He glanced toward the approaching vehicles and counted at least five steadily making their way through the vegetation.

He ran over to the others, who were just getting the two city dwellers under control. "Get up! We have to go. Now!"

Infinity slammed her forehead into one of the baseball-sized eyes of the lemur beneath her and jumped to her feet, leaving Vic to deal with the creature.

Gideon rolled away from Terry and the other lemur, grabbed his weapon off the forest floor, and rose beside Infinity. He took one look at the approaching vehicles and said, "You guys go! I'll slow them down."

The two city dwellers had now turned their attention to Vic and Terry, who were still struggling to disengage from the fight. "Goddammit!" Terry growled as he threw himself on top of one of the creatures and drove three rapid punches into its face. "These bastards don't give up!" He threw one more punch and then pulled away and got to his feet. He drew back his foot and delivered a full-force kick to the head of the lemur Vic was fighting and then grabbed Vic's arm and pulled him to his feet.

The vehicles were now spreading out to surround the humans.

"Go!" Gideon ordered. He raised his weapon and took aim at one of the robots.

A pop sounded. Gideon grunted. He dropped his gun and collapsed to his knees and then onto his back.

Desmond stared. Blood was gushing from Gideon's shoulder. His left arm was lying at an awkward angle, barely attached to his body by threads of shredded tissue.

Desmond's mind barely registered the sound of a blunt smack as Terry delivered one more blow to one of the lemurs on the ground.

Gideon groaned loudly as he rolled to his left side and pushed his weapon toward Infinity, who had knelt beside him. "One dart," he said. "Make it count."

She took the gun and looked up at the vehicles. "Don't worry, I will."

Vic's wrist translator began speaking, apparently interpreting the vocalizations from the approaching vehicles. "Do not fight. Stop. Put weapon down."

Desmond spun around. The humans were completely surrounded. He turned back to Infinity. She was now on her feet, glaring furiously at the city dwellers on vehicles. She was still holding Gideon's weapon down at her side, but the muscles in her arm rippled as she gripped it. Desmond knew without a doubt she would throw it to her shoulder and shoot within seconds if he didn't do something.

"Drop the gun, Infinity," he said. "You'll be dead the moment you aim it at them, and you know it."

Her chest heaved rhythmically and her nostrils flared.

Desmond glanced down at Gideon, who was no longer conscious, and then returned his gaze to Infinity. He tried not to envision numerous projectiles shredding her body. "Infinity, please. We need you alive."

She blinked. The muscles in her arm started to relax. The weapon tilted forward slightly as she loosened her grip. Then the gun dropped to the ground.

13

──────────

CAPTIVES

April 11 - 4:44 PM

INFINITY ARCHED her back and twisted her neck, trying to see Desmond—or any of the other humans. But the yellowish substance was restricting her movement to the point that it was difficult to breathe, let alone look around at her surroundings. There was little she could do except endure being tossed around by the vehicle's jerky gait as it made its way through the forest, presumably back toward the city.

She was behind one of the vehicles, suspended several feet off the ground by two mechanical appendages that had emerged from the rear of the machine's body. The appendages had obviously not been designed with the captive's comfort in mind.

The moment Infinity had dropped Gideon's weapon, she had been splattered with no fewer than four blobs of goo. After that, she had managed to catch a few glimpses of what was happening to her companions, and she had heard them shouting and cursing, but she had no idea whether Desmond or the two remaining Marines had been hurt in the struggle. And she had no idea whether Gideon was even still alive.

"If you hurt my friends, I swear I'll kill you all!" she shouted. But the city dwellers had removed her wrist translator, and she didn't know whether it could still hear her or whether it would translate her words, even if it could.

After Infinity had been jostled around for what felt like fifteen minutes, the vehicle stopped. She heard mechanical chittering near the front of the vehicle. The robot moved forward several steps, passing through a fence, then turned to the right. Strands of the yellow restraining substance were stretched across her face, but with one eye she was able to see two city dwellers leap from the robot and step over to the fence. One of them held the gap in the fence closed while the other used a black tool the size of a screwdriver to fuse the mesh back together.

Infinity twisted her body with all her strength, but it was useless—she couldn't break the substance's fibers. "Hey! I want to see my friends." The lemurs ignored her and got back on the vehicle. She twisted again. "You ugly bastards!"

The jostling resumed as she was carried through a shrubby field, perhaps the same field she and the others had run through the previous evening. The field gave way to the shantytown's pitiful shacks and piles of trash, and she was quickly overwhelmed by the odors of animal waste and rotting garbage. City dwellers in grimy white bodysuits spotted her and gathered around to walk beside the vehicle and gawk. They chattered excitedly until the vehicle riders barked at them, at which point they backed off. Soon another group had gathered, only to be chased off like the previous one. This same scenario occurred over and over as the vehicle made its way through what seemed like miles of filthy shanties. Infinity still saw no sign of Desmond or the others.

Finally, the vehicle stopped again. Peeking through the gaps in the restraining substance, Infinity could see only a handful of white-clad onlookers here, all keeping their distance. The two black-suited riders dismounted and stepped back beside Infinity. They stared silently at her.

"Give me my goddamn translator."

As always, their faces showed no expression, at least none she could recognize—just saucer-sized eyes ogling her, as if the creatures were no smarter than hamsters.

One of the lemurs extended a long finger, inserted it between the strands of Infinity's restraints, and gently poked one of her breasts through the organic material of her shirt. It purred and whistled softly, and then its companion replied with similar sounds.

The two creatures then grabbed Infinity's restraints and yanked her abruptly from the robot's appendages. She hit the ground with a thud, causing her to bite into her lower lip.

She was now lying on her back, looking up at a smooth, brown wall perhaps twenty-five feet high and extending into the distance. The city dwellers dragged her to the wall and then passed through an opening into a shadowy chamber. The door leading into the chamber must have closed because the area suddenly went from dim to almost entirely dark.

The two lemurs remained silent and continued dragging her, although it was too dark for her to make out any of the details of her surroundings. Her head hit something as she was hauled over a raised spot, and then the last hint of light disappeared.

In the inky blackness, Infinity felt the force of acceleration —she was in a vehicle of some kind.

The vehicle continued accelerating smoothly for at least a

minute. Then it turned sharply, and she slid to the side and hit a wall. Seconds later, another turn sent her sliding into the opposite wall. This went on for what felt like at least five minutes—accelerating, slowing, and turning one way or the other. Infinity was starting to worry that the cycle would never end when the vehicle began another turn, this time angling vertically, heading upward. She slid toward the back of the vehicle until her feet hit the wall, and soon she was actually standing, propped up awkwardly against a wall that had only seconds earlier been the floor. And all of this in total darkness.

The vehicle turned, leveling out again, and once again she was lying on her back.

Finally the vehicle came to a stop. Suddenly, without the warning of hinges squeaking or the rollers of a door opening, she saw flashes of light illuminating a large room, and she had to clamp her eyes shut against the brightness.

Hands gripped her restraints and dragged her a short distance before letting go. With eyes still shut, she heard the pattering of bare feet. Then silence.

She opened her eyes and squinted. Several figures were standing in front of her, at least five of them. She blinked a few times. Although bright light behind the figures made them little more than silhouettes, she could see that they were lemurs.

She blinked again. The light was coming through a huge window that stretched from floor to ceiling. The rest of the room was uniformly brown, the color of unfinished oak but without grain or texture. Infinity turned her head as far as she could. She saw a few more lemurs standing to one side, but otherwise the room was empty—no furniture or anything else.

One of the lemurs kneeled beside her and began cutting the strands of yellow stuff from her face with some kind of tool. The creature did this gently, removing all the pieces from her head and then wadding them into a tight ball and tossing it aside. She noticed four teats on the lemur's chest, pushing out against the creature's bodysuit.

Infinity's first inclination was to spit in the thing's face. Instead, she said, "Give me my translator so I can talk to you."

The lemur got to her feet and chattered back and forth with the others. More creatures joined in the conversation from someplace outside Infinity's field of vision, and she realized that the room was fuller than she had initially thought. As the creatures talked, she looked over the ones she could see. All were wearing solid black bodysuits that left only their heads, hands, and bare feet exposed. Each lemur also wore multiple colored bands on each ankle, more bands than Infinity had seen on any of the other city dwellers. Most of the creatures she could see had two bands of each color, one solid and the other with blue markings. The markings, as Grayface had explained it, were received for hunting and killing a lemur that was armed with a weapon of some kind. Infinity noted that several of the lemurs wore yellow bands—for killing ring-tails.

Another lemur stepped into view, kneeled, and held out Infinity's confiscated translator.

"That's it," Infinity said. "It's obviously not working now. Put it on my wrist." She tried motioning with her arm but the restraints made her movements look more like muscle spasms.

The lemurs chattered among themselves briefly, and then the one with the cutting tool returned and freed both Infinity's arms.

She pushed against the floor, sat up, and held out her hand for the translator. The lemur handed it to her, and Infinity slipped it on. She looked up at the creatures. "Now we should be able to talk. Assuming you haven't broken it."

A few seconds later, the device responded by converting her words to yelps, clicks, and whistles.

The lemurs stared at the translator for several long seconds.

Another figure stepped around from behind, and the others backed up slightly to make room. This lemur was a male, and he was noticeably stockier than the others in the room. He must have weighed at least 160 pounds, about thirty pounds more than Infinity. Also, he was wearing more colored ankle bands than any of the others. The bands on one of his legs, in fact, nearly covered the entire area below the knee.

Big Male sat down smoothly on his butt on the floor in front of Infinity. He calmly folded his legs and arranged them with the soles of his bare feet pressed together. He held out a sinewy finger, pointing at Infinity's translator, and spoke. When he was finished, the translator said, "That is interesting device. We do not have devices like that."

Infinity glanced at her wrist. "We don't have these either. They were given to us."

The lemur listened to the translation and then said, "Who gave them to you?"

Infinity shook her head. "First, I want to know where my friends are. I want you to show me that they're alive."

"The others of your species will be here soon. You will see."

"Your people shot one of my friends." Infinity put a hand over her left shoulder. "They shot him here. Is he alive?"

The lemur looked up at the others and they exchanged vocalizations. Infinity's translator remained silent. He then faced her again. "We do not know."

She studied his face. Was the bug-eyed bastard lying?

Big Male extended his finger again. This time he poked

one of her breasts. "Show me you are a female. Show me now."

Infinity glared at him and fought back the urge to punch his face. But that would only get her killed. In fact, refusing to comply might also get her killed. She gritted her teeth and picked off some of the remaining yellow strands on her shirt. She pulled the shirt up and exposed one of her breasts. "I'm a female. Maybe you should have to show me that you're a male." Infinity couldn't care less, but her anger was getting the best of her.

The lemur listened to the translation and then casually pointed to his bumpless chest. He then pointed to his crotch, where a bulge the size and shape of a peanut shell was visible beneath the black fabric of his bodysuit.

Infinity considered making a demeaning joke but thought better of it. Instead, she silently decided to change his name from Big Male to Peanut.

Peanut spoke again. "You are a female. The others of your species are males. Tell me where to get more females of your species."

She laughed. "Sorry, you're out of luck. I'm the only one. And you know what's really funny? I can't make babies! I guess this just isn't your day."

Peanut stared at her as he listened to the translation. He then spoke to someone behind Infinity. She turned to look as the lemur came around and kneeled beside her. This creature was wearing a contraption in the form of a vest. The device was mostly black with nine rounded nodules arranged in rows of three across the lemur's chest and abdomen. A tube or cable ran from each side of the device down the length of each of the lemur's arms, ending in a rectangular block held in the creature's fingers. The lemur motioned for Infinity to lift her shirt again.

She was actually curious now, so she complied and raised her shirt about six inches.

The lemur leaned in closer and placed one of the blocks against her belly and the other against her lower back, opposite the first block. Everyone in the room remained silent as the creature slowly moved the blocks back and forth and then up and down, apparently scanning for something. The device wasn't making any sound, and as far as Infinity could tell there was no screen or readout to look at.

The lemur continued moving the blocks around for a minute or so and then pulled them back and got to its feet. It turned to the others and spoke to them.

While the creature was still talking, Peanut barked abruptly. He then spun to the side and kicked the examiner in the gut, and the creature doubled over, struggling to catch its breath. Peanut threw himself on top of his victim and within seconds had locked his legs around the examiner's neck, using the same scissor chokehold the juvenile ring-tails had demonstrated earlier in the day.

The helpless examiner gasped for air but otherwise barely even fought back. The other lemurs in the room were shifting nervously but doing nothing to intervene.

The room was completely silent except for the sounds of the examiner's pained choking. The pitiful gasps became weaker as the creature began to die.

Suddenly, Peanut released the examiner and got to his feet.

The smaller lemur sat up, frantically sucking in oxygen. It crawled to the other side of the room and leaned back against the wall.

Infinity watched the terrified creature for a moment and then turned back to Peanut. "What just happened? What did he say to you?"

Peanut had walked over to the expansive window and was staring out. When the translation ended, he turned around and spoke. "I want to know where I can get more females of your species. Tell me what I want to know."

"What did he say to you?" Infinity repeated. She knew she was probably about to die, but she felt an overwhelming need to know what the examiner had said. What had the creature seen while examining her? Had it confirmed what she had suspected ever since she'd been stabbed in the abdomen by Eddy Chastain at sixteen? "Tell me what he said, goddammit!"

Scuffling, dragging sounds came from behind her. Infinity turned. Two lemurs were dragging a bound body into the room through a dark doorway. They dropped the body, and its head thumped the floor. One of the new lemurs handed a wrist translator to Peanut then quickly stepped back through the doorway. Then, without a sound, the doorway simply disappeared. One second, it had been a dark hole in the wall, and the next second, the wall was solid again.

The bound figure moaned and rolled to one side. A face shifted behind a mask of yellow bindings until one eye was peering out at Infinity. It was Vic. "Good to see you ain't dead," he said.

"Good to see you too, Vic. Have you seen the others? Is Desmond okay?"

"Ain't seen much of anything. They dragged my ass all over the place, but all I seen was the ground and a bunch of filthy lemurs."

The door appeared again. This time four lemurs entered dragging two bound bodies. The creatures dropped the bodies, handed over two more translators, and withdrew. The door disappeared.

"Infinity!"

Infinity exhaled—one of the figures was Desmond. The other was Terry. "I'm okay," she said, dispensing with greetings in spite of her relief. "They've been questioning me. You'll probably get the same treatment. I suggest you cooperate. Definitely don't piss off the big guy. He's got a temper."

"Duly noted," Desmond said. "What about Gideon? Is he alive?"

"They say they don't know."

The lemur who had cut Infinity free began making its way from one new arrival to the next, cutting the restraining substance from their faces and arms. As with Infinity, the creature left their legs completely bound. Peanut tossed each of them a wrist translator. Desmond shot Infinity a quizzical look.

"Go ahead and put it on," she said. "It seems they want to talk."

Peanut stepped over to Vic and gazed down at him for a moment. The creature then crouched and roughly groped the Marine's chest and crotch. He stood back up and spoke. Vic's translator said, "You are a male." The lemur repeated the same process with Terry and then Desmond.

"Do I even want to know what he's doing?" asked Desmond as Peanut was finishing his examination.

"I'm pretty sure he wants to start breeding us," she said. "He's upset that I'm the only female."

Terry shifted his body, trying to find a comfortable position for his bound legs. "The assholes want to hunt humans for sport. I hope you told them to go to hell."

Infinity didn't feel like explaining that she'd been more focused on what the lemur with the examining device had learned, so she didn't reply.

Peanut spoke, and Infinity's translator said, "Tell us where we can find more females of your species."

Infinity sighed forcefully. "I've already told you. There aren't any more. Not anywhere in this entire universe. We came here from a completely different universe, and there's no way you can ever get there." Her device began translating for the lemur, and she turned to Desmond, Vic, and Terry. "These sadistic bastards can *never* get their hands on bridging technology."

They all three nodded. Desmond said, "It'd be like unleashing a plague."

Infinity turned back to Peanut and realized the creature was eyeing her. Peanut then began speaking to the other lemurs, and a wave of uncertainty washed over Infinity. Had her device translated the words she'd said to Desmond, thinking she was still talking to the lemur?

Peanut placed his fingertips on the floor and moved his face closer to Infinity's until he was no more than a foot away. He stared at her for a moment, studying her eyes, and then spoke. "If the words you say are true, then we cannot obtain more of your species. If we cannot obtain more of your species, then you are not worth keeping. If you are not worth keeping, then we will hunt you in the course... field... arena."

Infinity glanced down at her translator. Apparently it had struggled to come up with an accurate translation.

The lemur raised himself back up to his full height and spoke briefly to the other lemurs. He then gazed at the four humans, his eyes moving from one person to the next, lingering on each of them for several seconds. Finally, he extended his arm and pointed a finger at Terry.

Two of the lemurs immediately sprung into action, grabbing Terry by the feet and dragging him to the wall.

"What?" Terry sputtered. "What are you doing?"

The doorway in the wall silently appeared. Two other

lemurs stepped out from the darkness beyond and dragged Terry from the room.

Terry started to struggle. "What the hell, man? Why can't I—"

The doorway vanished, cutting off his words.

Infinity twisted her head around and shouted at Peanut. "This is how you treat people who visit your city? If you hurt one more of my friends, our people are going to come here and destroy your entire goddamn civilization!"

The lemur listened to the translation. Then he casually circled her until he was standing in front of her. He crouched down, putting his face inches from hers, and said, "You speak interesting words. We would be very happy if your people came here and tried to destroy our civilization. I hope that the words you speak are true." He waited for the translation to end, stood up, and spoke again. "I will now explain more about us and our city." He motioned to someone behind Infinity.

Lemurs came forward, dragged her, Desmond, and Vic across the room, and deposited them in front of the expansive window.

Infinity couldn't help but stare. She had never been in a building taller than a ten-story apartment building. Now she found herself looking down upon the lemur city from at least a quarter mile up—maybe even higher. The landscape below was segmented into three distinct areas. Arranged in a miles-wide half-circle beneath her was a modern-looking city, with hundreds of gleaming, cylindrical buildings, the tallest of which was only half as tall as the one she was looking down from. Beyond the city was a band of brownish-gray, haphazard shacks, interspersed with vast, smoking trash piles and blocky structures that appeared to be factories. Beyond all that was green forest stretching to the horizon—the enclosures for the various lemur species the city dwellers hunted for sport.

Peanut began speaking again. Desmond's translator began interpreting while the creature was still talking—apparently this was going to be a long speech. "Surely you must see that our civilization is extraordinary. We are more powerful and successful than all the other intelligent, speaking species. The other species provide us with honor and with fun. The other species also provide us with much more than honor and fun. They provide us with order... lawfulness... obedience. I will now explain."

Desmond's translator paused for about ten seconds and then resumed. "Hunting the other species for honor and fun is what we all wish to do. But only some of us have the wealth to be able to hunt the other species. The others do not have such wealth. That is the way it must be, because only a limited amount of wealth can exist. But we must give hope to those without wealth. We must give them a reason to continue working. We give them opportunities to hunt, but only if they continue to work, only if they continue to serve the city."

The lemur paused and waited until the translator finished. He then began talking again as he pointed out the window at the expansive green forests beyond the slums. "Those are enclosures we built for the other intelligent species. Many of our wealthy hunt and kill in those enclosures, for honor and for fun. Only our wealthiest can hunt in the enclosures."

He paused as the translator caught up. He pointed out the window again, this time toward a wide, sprawling structure among the gleaming buildings below. Infinity didn't see any streets crisscrossing the city, but she guessed the massive structure would cover at least ten blocks of a human city.

Desmond's translator resumed its interpretation. "That is

our course... field... arena. It is essential to the functioning of our city, for it is where those without wealth hope someday to have the honor of hunting and killing. Most of them will never achieve such honor, but it is important that they have hope of achieving it. When they have hope for it, they continue to work for it, and they continue to serve our city. We allow them to watch the hunts that take place there. Watching the hunts makes them desire someday to achieve their own hunt."

The lemur trained his wide eyes directly on Infinity. "Now you will watch a hunt in our arena. Those in our city without wealth have finished their work for the day and will watch also. They will see what you see, and they will work even harder tomorrow, hoping to be selected for the next hunt. This hunt will be special. Do you know why this hunt will be special?" He continued staring at Infinity as the translation finished, and then he waited.

Infinity glared back at him, seething with anger. She wasn't going to give him the satisfaction of a response.

Finally, Vic spoke up. "If you like fighting so much, cut this shit off my legs. I'll choke you with your own tail and throw your body through this window."

Peanut stared at Vic as he listened to the translation. He then replied, and Vic's device translated. "You speak interesting words. Perhaps you are a child. Or perhaps your head is damaged. It makes no difference. You will fight soon. We will choose one who has no wealth to hunt and kill you. You will be easy to kill, but your death will still bring honor to one who has no wealth."

Infinity glanced at Desmond. He shook his head, cautioning her to keep her mouth shut. She turned back to Peanut in time to see him watching Desmond intently. Had the creature understood Desmond's gesture? It seemed unlikely, but then she really had no idea how intelligent these lemurs might be.

Peanut nodded, and several other lemurs came forward and dragged the three humans back from the window to their previous location. Apparently story time was over.

Peanut addressed the humans again. "This hunt will be special because one without wealth will hunt and kill a new intelligent species—a species we have not hunted before. The others without wealth will enjoy this very much, and they will work very hard tomorrow. Perhaps you will enjoy watching this hunt too."

Peanut gestured to one of the other lemurs, and a few seconds later the window to the outside transformed into a viewing screen. Not only was the screen floor-to-ceiling and wall-to-wall, but its image was also bright and sharp, as good as any television Infinity had ever seen. She realized she was looking at the inside of a room with brown walls, similar to the room she was in now.

A few seconds passed, and then two black-clad city dwellers stepped into view. They were dragging a struggling figure—Terry. The Marine's legs were still bound by the yellow substance, and it looked like another ball of goo had splattered his upper body because his arms were once again entangled. Only his head was unrestrained. He was shouting, and every one of his words was coming through the video feed loud and clear.

"Where are you taking me? Goddammit, take me back to the others!"

Infinity could hear the fear in the young man's voice, and she felt a new, intense rage building inside her.

The lemurs stopped dragging him. One of them kneeled and cut away just enough of the yellow substance to free one of his hands. The creature then placed the cutting tool into

Terry's free hand, and the two lemurs backed out of the picture.

The screen cut to a view from another camera, this one closer to Terry's face, close enough to see his beard stubble and the moisture in the corners of his eyes. "Where you going?" he demanded. "What am I supposed to do with this?"

Lemur vocalizations came over the video as the camera panned over the Marine's body. Perhaps the narrator was attempting to explain to the viewing audience what kind of creature they were looking at.

The screen cut again to another camera, this one showing the entire room, with Terry lying in the middle of the floor. The far wall beyond Terry suddenly transformed into a screen showing a vast area of trees and boulders. But the area obviously wasn't a natural forest—Infinity could see a flat, artificial floor between the clumps of trees and rocks, and a brown ceiling above stretched into the distance. She then realized this wasn't another video screen at all, but rather an opening into a much larger chamber—the arena.

"Oh, man," Terry said. "What the hell is this?"

The screen cut to a camera focused on Terry's free hand. He had dropped the cutting tool, and now he was frantically groping for it. His hand found it. The tool looked like nothing more than a brown piece of plastic with a point at one end. He turned it over in his hand and started cutting at the strands binding his other arm.

The lemur voice on the video feed continued talking, but Infinity's translator remained silent.

A few seconds later, Terry had freed both his arms and was working on his legs. The screen continued cutting to different camera angles, each showing different details of the Marine's struggle to free himself. These camera changes were obviously intended to ratchet up the drama. Infinity imagined thousands of lemurs watching this situation unfold, eager for the hunt to begin. She had encountered such violent and ruthless beings during her bridging career, but never in an advanced society like this.

Terry finished cutting away his bindings. Still sitting on the floor, he stared at the cutting tool in his hand. Then—surprisingly—he tossed it aside. He got to his feet. The camera followed him as he moved to one side of the room and began slamming his fists against the brown wall. "Come back, goddammit! I'm not going in there."

Infinity thought she saw movement and blinked. She hadn't imagined it—the wall in front of Terry was now moving. No, not just the wall. The entire room was shifting, becoming smaller, forcing him toward the arena. He kept pounding the wall, but it was useless. Seconds later the room was gone, and he was standing with his back to the wall. The screen cut to a camera showing the arena before him. The landscape was dominated by smooth-floored trails winding among clusters of trees and brush-covered mounds of various heights—a seemingly-endless obstacle course for a cruel game.

The screen cut again to another camera, this one showing a city dweller in a torn and stained body suit that at one time may have been white. The creature was creeping steadily through the maze of trails, looking cautiously from side to side. This was obviously the lucky hunter—the lemur without wealth chosen over all the others to hunt and kill. For fun. And for honor. Whatever the hell that meant.

The hunting lemur stopped and peered at something ahead. The screen cut to a view from above, apparently from a camera on the arena's ceiling. Infinity located Terry and clenched her teeth—the hunter was no more than fifty yards from him and was creeping closer by the second.

"Private Epsom!" Vic cried out. "Look to your right. Dammit, look!"

Not surprisingly, Terry didn't respond. Infinity glanced at Peanut. The bastard was gazing at Vic, perhaps more interested in the human's reaction than what was happening on the screen.

The hunter suddenly bolted, running on all fours directly toward the Marine. The screen cut to a camera at ground level, amplifying the drama of the charge.

"Epsom!" Vic shouted again.

Terry spotted the approaching hunter. "Oh shit," he muttered, his words clearly audible over the video feed. He turned and ran. He made it to the nearest cluster of trees, but by that time the lemur was almost on top of him. The creature dove for the Marine's feet and tackled him. The screen cut to a closer camera as Terry went down. The lemur began executing what appeared to be an overly-elaborate set of grappling moves, spinning its body several times, perhaps hoping to cause confusion, and then wrapping its legs around Terry's to immobilize them. The creature then attempted to bite Terry's neck.

But the hunter had obviously practiced these moves on other lemurs, who were much smaller than the Marine. Terry was a big guy, easily 200 pounds, at least seventy pounds heavier than his attacker. And the Marine, although terrified, was obviously no stranger to fighting. The hunter gnashed its teeth but couldn't quite reach Terry's neck. Grunting and cursing, Terry clutched the lemur's throat and pushed away its gaping mouth. He then flung his knees up and used his momentum to roll over on top of the lemur.

Vic was now straining at the substance binding his legs. "Do it, Epsom! Kill the son of a bitch!"

The view cut to a closer camera no more than a few yards

from the struggle. Terry straight-armed the lemur's throat against the floor. The creature kicked its legs wildly, grunting and gasping for air as it tried to grab Terry's face with its hands. But the Marine's arm was too long.

Terry snarled something unintelligible, the raw fear in his voice unmistakable. He drew back his free arm and drove his palm into the creature's face, remembering at least enough of his training to use his open palm instead of breaking his knuckles using a balled fist. He quickly struck the lemur again, and then again.

"That's it, man," Vic said. "Do it. Do it again."

Terry kept striking, over and over, and soon Vic trailed off and fell silent. The high-def image on the screen showed every bit of blood and splattering eyeball fluid in crystal-clear detail. Terry's growls gradually became sobs, but still he didn't stop. Finally, long after there could be any doubt the lemur was dead, the Marine released the mangled creature and got to his feet. His chest heaved as he caught his breath.

The room around Infinity was completely silent. Peanut had now turned his attention back to the screen and was fixated on it.

"I want to go back to my team," Terry cried out, looking up at the arena's ceiling. "Did you hear me? Take me back to my team!"

Peanut gestured with one arm, and the video feed abruptly disappeared, replaced again by the window overlooking the city and the forest beyond. The lemur began talking, and Infinity's translator interpreted. "This hunt was very interesting, although it did not bring honor to the hunter. Your species is interesting. Our people have reported that you killed some of our species in the enclosure beyond our city. At first I did not believe such words could be true. But now I see the words may indeed be true. I would like very much for you to tell me where I can get more of your species. But you say it is not possible. Those are interesting words. I am not sure I can believe such words are true. This is an interesting problem."

Peanut then extended his arm and pointed at Desmond. Two of the other lemurs came forward, picked up Desmond's feet, and began dragging him toward the wall.

"No!" Infinity shrieked. "Take me instead. He's not a fighter. But I am. You want entertainment? Honor? Then take me, goddammit!"

The lemurs ignored her, and she began struggling, fighting to get the restraining fibers off her legs. She somehow managed to get to her feet. She launched herself at Peanut. He stepped back just in time, and she fell to the floor. She rolled toward him, threw her right arm around his ankle, and then pulled his foot toward her until it was off the floor. She then used the leverage gained from this motion to whip her bound legs around and kick his other foot from under him. He went down, but he overcame his surprise in a split second and spread his arms and legs into a sprawl, securing his position above her. She pulled his ankle closer and bit down on his calf, but she didn't get much more than a mouthful of fur.

A fist slammed into her temple, tearing her teeth from the leg and causing her head to bounce off the floor.

She clenched her eyes shut until the pain started to subside and she began to regain her senses. By the time she opened them again, Peanut was back on his feet and standing clear of her reach.

"I'm the fighter you want," she said, glaring up at him. "Take me instead."

The lemur stood perfectly still as he listened to the translation.

"Infinity," Desmond said from across the room, his voice

as calm as ever. "Please stop. If we talk reasonably with them, maybe we can get them to see that there's value in keeping us alive."

She rolled onto her belly and got to her knees. "You know that's not going to happen. These bastards aren't capable of thinking the way you do."

Peanut gestured to the lemurs who had dragged Desmond, and they hauled him back to his original location and dropped his feet. Peanut then lowered himself until his fingers were resting on the floor, still maintaining a safe distance from Infinity. He leveled his gaze at her and spoke. "Your words are interesting, and your words are humorous. Yes, you will be hunted in the arena. It will be a very interesting hunt. Each day, we have one hunt that is the most important hunt of the day. Now the most important hunt for today will be your hunt. This hunt will be very special because I will be the hunter. I will hunt and kill you, and all those without wealth and all those with wealth will watch."

The lemur waited for the translation to end. He then pointed to the colored bands on one of his ankles and continued speaking. "Tonight I will earn a band. The band will have a new color. I will be the first of my kind to earn a band of this color."

14

____

COWARD

APRIL 11 - 7:29 PM

DESMOND USED to consider himself a coward, with a talent for avoiding conflict. But then he had met Infinity and had become a bridger, and everything had gone to hell. Since then, he had narrowly escaped death more times than he cared to remember. So he had gradually started to believe he wasn't a coward after all. But now he knew better.

Infinity had acted decisively, fearlessly, attempting to sacrifice herself to save him—like a soldier throwing herself onto a grenade. Desmond's initial reaction to her attempt had been disbelief. And then despair. But there was no denying the fact that another feeling had briefly surfaced—relief. He had felt a wave of relief when he realized he wasn't immediately going to be taken to the arena.

Desmond closed his eyes and rubbed his temples. It was a waste of time and energy to dwell on feelings he had no control over. Instead, he needed to focus and be ready to act, to do whatever he could to disrupt the current course of events.

"I'm right, and you know I am," Infinity said.

Of course he knew she was right. "No, you're not right," he replied. "You're not *always* right. Baiting him into a fight to the death was reckless. There has to be a better way. Even if you manage to kill him, they'll just send in another hunter, and another after that. They intend to hunt and kill all of us."

"I don't know about that."

Desmond gazed at her. "What do you mean?"

She glanced around the room as if she were concerned about eavesdroppers. The big male—the one who seemed to be in charge—had left some minutes ago, probably to prepare for the hunt. Only a handful of lemurs had remained to keep watch over the humans. She turned back to him. "I'm pretty sure Peanut thinks we're hiding something. I think his goal is to get one of us to tell him where he can find more humans."

Desmond shook his head, exasperated. "It doesn't matter. He's going to hunt you and try to kill you. Yes, he's right, I'll say whatever I have to say to save your life, but nothing I can say will give him access to more humans. I can't produce what he wants!"

She gazed at him, expressionless. "You sure about that?"

He frowned. What was she getting at?

"Look," she said. "Our best move is to use the skills we have. We both know you're smarter than me. I should be in the arena fighting Peanut, and you should be here. You figured out how to control the robot vehicle—you'll figure out how to negotiate with these assholes."

He sighed. She was giving his abilities far too much credit. "Why do you call him Peanut, anyway?"

The corner of her mouth curled up slightly. "The name suits him."

The doorway suddenly appeared in the wall. Two lemurs dragged Terry into the room and roughly dropped him. He was bound again from his neck to his feet.

Vic used his arms to scoot himself until he was beside his fellow Marine. "You did it, brother. You killed the son of a bitch. With your bare hands."

Terry was trying to sit up, but his arms were still bound, and he ended up on his side. He blinked at Vic. "How do you know that?"

"We saw the whole thing, man. In high definition. You're one hell of a Marine, brother."

Terry stared silently at the floor for a moment. "Help me sit up. I could use a little dignity."

Vic called over to the lemurs. "Hey, could you free his hands please?"

One of the lemurs replied, "We do not want to free his hands."

Vic mumbled something and pulled Terry up to a sitting position. Vic then helped him scoot several feet to the wall, where the bound Marine could lean back.

Terry nodded in appreciation. "This isn't what I signed up for—being hunted like an animal." He then pursed his lips and closed his eyes.

Infinity said, "Terry, you did what you had to do. Damn good job."

Terry opened his eyes and gave her a glassy stare. Finally, he nodded slightly.

Infinity nudged Desmond. "It'll be my turn soon. Remember, our goal here isn't merely to survive. We're here to save Vic and Terry's world. If we screw this up, Armando and the rest of our family will die along with everyone else on the planet."

Desmond considered this for a few seconds. "Doesn't mean I'm ready to lose you."

The doorway appeared again. Two lemurs stepped into the room, each holding what looked like a fat PVC pipe. They immediately pointed the pipes at Infinity and shot her with softball-sized blobs of yellow goo, which burst on contact, entangling the upper half of her body. She grunted with each impact but didn't bother to struggle.

"Desmond, they'll be ready to listen to what you have to say!" she shouted as the lemurs grabbed her and dragged her through the doorway into the darkness beyond. The door disappeared, leaving only the oak-colored wall.

Desmond inhaled deeply. He'd been hiding his anxiety to reassure Infinity that he was worthy of her sacrifice. What if he *wasn't* worthy? What if he couldn't come up with anything to say to the lemurs that would make any difference? He rubbed his scalp, thinking furiously. Several possibilities came to him, but what if he chose one that made things worse? There was simply no way to know without trying. He had to do something.

Desmond waved his arm at the lemurs in the room to get their attention. "I need to talk to someone in charge. Now!"

The lemurs listened to his translator's interpretation, and then one of them approached him but remained out of his reach. The creature spoke briefly. "If you will speak words that are true, I will listen."

Desmond looked the creature over. Although not as imposing as Peanut, this lemur, a female, wore almost as many colored bands on her ankles. And she was larger than any of the other lemurs in the room. She'd have to do.

"I understand what you want," Desmond said. "You want more humans like us—more of our species. You want enough to start breeding us. Well, what I can give you is something much better than that."

The lemur listened to the translation and then said, "Continue speaking your words. I will listen."

"First I need to know that if I give you what you want, you will stop the hunt and let me and my friends live. In fact, we'd like to live comfortably. We'd like a place to stay and some of your wealth."

"What are you doing, man?" Vic asked as Desmond's words were being translated.

Desmond held up a hand to silence him. "Just trust me."

The lemur spoke. "Yes, if you tell us where to get more of your species, we will not hunt you. We will make you wealthy and comfortable."

Good enough. Desmond had no idea how long it was supposed to be before Peanut began hunting Infinity, but he wanted to stop the hunt before it could even get started. He spoke to the lemur again. "We bridged to this world from another universe. There are an infinite number of universes. I don't know if your species is aware of this, but it's true. There is a different universe for every possible arrangement of quantum particles. That means there are other versions of this world—infinite versions. Many of those versions have others of our species, humans. Many other versions have different intelligent species. Different intelligent species for you to hunt and kill for honor and fun. More species than you could ever imagine." He paused to allow the translator to catch up.

"Hey, man," said Vic, "I thought we agreed—"

Desmond held up his hand again. "Be careful what you say—our translators might be picking up more than we think they are. Please just trust me, okay?"

Vic frowned, but then he nodded. Terry, still leaning against the wall, was now watching Desmond intently.

"Your words are interesting," the lemur said. "Continue speaking."

Desmond went on. "All of these infinite universes exist. All of these different intelligent species exist. But your species will never be able to bridge back and forth between universes. Because you don't have the technology—the device—that would allow you to bridge. My species has this technology." Again he paused until the translation finished.

The lemur stared at him with her perpetually-round eyes, apparently waiting for more.

Desmond said, "This bridging technology was given to my species, and we can give it to you. But only if you stop this hunt now and let us all live."

After the translation ended, the female lemur spoke briefly to the other lemurs in the room. She then turned back to Desmond. "You must prove that you have such an ability."

Desmond cursed silently. He had hoped that he could buy Infinity some time by convincing the lemurs he could provide something he couldn't actually provide. But these creatures were apparently familiar with the concept of lying. "I obviously can't prove it to you at this moment," he said to the lemur. "It will take time. Stop the hunt so that we can begin the process."

The creature listened to the translation and then answered without hesitating. "Your words are no longer interesting."

Seconds later, the vast window became a viewing screen once again. Desmond turned and stared. The screen showed Peanut in brilliant detail standing among a few of the clumps of trees in the arena, engaged in some kind of warm-up ritual. Announcer-style lemur vocalizations came over the video feed, no doubt serving to build anticipation among the viewing audience. Peanut spun around, kicked, and rolled on the ground. The movements were almost like a dance, and Desmond guessed it was the lemur's way of showing off, perhaps another way to build the audience's excitement.

Desmond's gut started to knot up. He tapped the video camera embedded in his forehead and spoke aloud. "Kitty, if you're still watching, please listen to me. Surely by now you've seen enough to make your judgement about us. It's time to stop this, before every last one of us is dead. Please bridge all of us back now!"

Nothing.

The screen in front of him cut to a different view, a now-familiar room with brown walls. Two lemurs entered the frame, dragging Infinity's bound body. They stopped near the center of the room. One of them cut away a few strands of the goo and placed the cutting tool in Infinity's hand. Then they both promptly backed out of view.

It was time for the hunt.

15

———

ARENA

APRIL 11 - 8:07 PM

INFINITY RAN her fingers over the tool in her hand—it was smooth and triangular, and one of its edges was sharpened near the narrowest point. She turned it around and dug at the binding substance with the tip until it was under at least one of the strands. She then sawed back and forth, and the strands broke almost immediately. This gave her more freedom to maneuver, and she began severing more strands. The yellow, hardened goo, which was seemingly impossible to break by pulling, turned out to be ridiculously easy to cut. Soon her entire right arm was free, and she started working on her left arm. Less than a minute later, she had freed her entire body.

She got to her feet, still gripping the cutting tool. Suddenly she felt the tool begin to change in her hand, becoming softer. By the time she held it up to stare at it, the tool was drooping, like a slice of brown, melting cheese. No wonder Terry had left his behind. She tossed the now-worth-less blob aside and waited for the door to the arena to appear, tensing her muscles and clearing her mind. She knew Desmond and the others were watching, but she was determined not to allow that to affect her decisions once the hunt began.

Finally, one of the room's walls disappeared, exposing her to the arena beyond. The arena was larger than it had looked on the screen. The brown ceiling above stretched so far into the distance that she couldn't see the far walls. Good—the more space she had, the easier it would be for her to stall and give Desmond the time he would need.

Infinity didn't wait for the room around her to begin shrinking. She started running.

Once in the arena, she cut to her left, remembering that Terry's hunter had approached from the right. The brushy mounds and clusters of trees were too small to hide in, which was probably by design. After all, a hunt that dragged on for hours wouldn't make good entertainment. Based on what she'd seen so far, the audience expected immediate engagement. Well, this time they'd be disappointed.

Assuming Peanut was already positioned near the room where she'd been released, Infinity made sure to stay positioned so that several obstacles were blocking her line of sight back in that general direction at all times.

After she had run several hundred yards, she stopped and pushed her way into a cluster of trees. The cluster was no more than ten feet in diameter, and only two of the trees stood taller than her head. None were large enough to climb. Up close she could see that the trees and shrubs weren't even real. The leaves were stiff, perhaps made of some kind of plastic. The trunks were smooth, with patterns of bark and ridges printed on them. Just enough to look real on a video screen.

Infinity crouched in the fake vegetation and scanned her

surroundings. The other tree clusters were similar to this one, perhaps even identical. The brushy mounds, on the other hand, were of various heights, but she couldn't see any that would offer much concealment. Her best bet was to keep as much distance between herself and Peanut as possible.

A movement caught her eye, something black. There it was again, something shuffling between two mounds. Suddenly Peanut came into view, about halfway back to her point of release. He was moving directly toward her.

How was this possible? Infinity could think of only two explanations—either Peanut had a bloodhound's nose, or he was getting some kind of assistance.

"They're cheating," she said aloud, knowing Desmond and the Marines could hear every word. Infinity hadn't seen any cameras but knew several would be focused on her at all times. "Maybe you can shame them into making this a fair fight."

She ducked out of the cluster and started running, keeping low.

She made it about two hundred yards and then ducked behind a mound, trying to stay quiet as she sucked in lungfuls of warm, humid air. Peering out, she saw no sign of Peanut pursuing her, but she was certain the bastard was coming. She needed to keep moving. She readied herself to run again but then hesitated, closing her eyes briefly. She cursed silently and then struggled out of her now-damp organic shirt. She kicked off her shoes, removed her trousers, and then put the shoes back on. Much better. The air against her skin was cooling, and she'd be able to move more easily.

She scanned the area and spotted the lemur moving steadily toward her. His casual, upright stride made it clear that he was not tracking her by scent.

Infinity tossed her clothes into the brush covering the

mound. She took off running again, naked except for the shoes on her feet and feeling more agile and confident.

After running for no more than ten seconds, she stopped. Less than a hundred yards ahead was a brown wall, extending to the ceiling high above. She couldn't possibly have run all the way to the far end of the arena. The place was at least a mile long. She looked to the left. There was a wall there too, this one even closer, and another to the right.

"The bastards are boxing me in," she said, although at this point she was pretty sure Desmond wasn't going to have much luck convincing the lemurs to allow a fair fight.

The wall to her right was more distant than the others so she headed toward it at a sprint. Suddenly, in half the time it should've taken, she found herself directly in front of the wall. She skidded to a stop and pounded it with her fist. It was definitely solid—not an illusion. Apparently the lemurs wanted to watch a fight, not a chase. But how could they possibly have moved a wall this size without making a sound?

Infinity turned and scanned the arena. The other walls were definitely moving closer. No sign of Peanut yet, but he couldn't be far. She moved to the nearest cluster of fake trees. The smaller stalks gave way as she pushed past them and climbed to the cluster's center. She yanked on a stalk that was about two inches thick, but she couldn't detach it from the floor. She tried a smaller one. This one came loose immediately. Three grass-like leaves were protruding from the end of the stalk, but she was able to tear them off like tissue paper. The tip turned out to be pointed—a pleasant surprise. The point wasn't super sharp, but sharp enough. Just as important, the stalk was reasonably straight and had some heft. What the hell? The lemurs didn't want her to use the little cutting tool, but they provide a sharpened, three-foot stick?

As Infinity kneeled down in the center of the cluster to

wait, it occurred to her that the longer weapon would be more visible to the audience, making for a more entertaining conflict. Also, giving the victims a chance to acquire weapons would give the hunters a chance to earn ankle bands with blue markings. Infinity tightened her grip on the weapon and allowed her disgust to fan the flames of her hatred for the city dwellers. If Peanut wanted to earn a band tonight, he'd have to work for it.

She spotted him through the trees, still moving steadily toward her.

Infinity backed out of the cluster of plants and made herself as small as she could. The plants were sparse, and she'd be better concealed with the entire cluster between her and Peanut.

The lemur kept coming. He was carrying no weapons that Infinity could see, but she knew better than to underestimate his skill. At about fifty yards out and still walking toward her, he began looking warily from side to side, as if he didn't know where she was. Infinity suspected this was bullshit. He had followed almost exactly in her footsteps for at least a quarter mile without straying. He knew exactly where she was. He stopped walking at about fifteen yards out. He continued glancing from side to side, but the range of glances became narrower, until finally he was staring in her direction.

Infinity ran dozens of battle scenarios through her mind, both offensive and defensive, but it was still too early to choose one. Her move would depend on what Peanut did next.

The lemur slowly lowered his head and upper body until the fingers of his left hand were resting on the floor. He raised his right arm, elbow out, and clenched his fist beside his cheek. His tail fluttered a few times above his back.

Infinity had already suspected this fight stance was pure

bravado, and now she was sure of it. The asshole was posturing for his audience.

Infinity spoke aloud to Desmond. "I can't drag this out any longer. I hope you're making progress up there."

Peanut was close enough to have easily heard her voice, but at this point it didn't matter. The lemur remained still, as if he expected her to come charging out and attack him. But Infinity had no intention of playing his game, a game he had obviously mastered.

Suddenly, she had an idea. She rose to her full height and pushed her way back to the center of the cluster of fake vegetation, where she was again surrounded by rigid stalks on all sides. She looked out at Peanut and said, "Come get me." Her translator, which had been silent since she had entered the arena, emitted a brief sequence of whistles.

The lemur stared back at her and blinked his massive eyes once. He spoke, and her translator interpreted. "You have said that you are a fighter. Perhaps you spoke words that were not true."

Infinity was tempted to taunt the bastard, but she knew that would only piss him off and speed things up rather than buy Desmond more time. She remained silent.

Peanut waited a few more seconds and then rose to his feet. He approached her slowly and walked around the plant cluster's perimeter. Infinity turned her body to continue facing him. She tried to keep her weapon hidden at her side.

Suddenly, Peanut's posture shifted, indicating he was about to attack.

Infinity tensed her muscles but didn't raise her weapon.

The lemur plunged into the cluster of stalks, knocking them aside ferociously with his elbows.

A few seconds later, he was within reach. Infinity raised her weapon and thrust it into his throat in one fluid motion.

She looked at the weapon. She thought she'd felt the shaft sink several inches into his throat. But now she saw that the stick's tip was drooping loosely. She pulled it back, and it swung like a soggy noodle.

The weapon was rigged. But it was too late to change her strategy—the lemur was upon her. Fake plant stalks whipped about and clacked against each other as Peanut ducked low and struggled to throw his arms around her waist. But his right arm was entangled in the stalks. Infinity swung her weapon like a club, striking his back with all her strength. This time the entire stalk softened upon impact, but the momentum was still substantial enough that the weapon made a loud *whack*.

Infinity dropped the weapon and threw a hard right down upon the lemur's head. Peanut finally yanked his right arm free of the stalks and thrust it around her waist. He started reaching around with his other hand, but Infinity spun to her right and pulled free before he could lock his fingers together. He stumbled and went down onto all fours. She immediately slammed an elbow onto the back of his head. The hit was solid, sending a wave of pain through her shoulder.

Infinity stumbled out of the tree cluster and started running. She estimated she had five seconds before Peanut recovered and came after her. She glanced over her shoulder. She had been wrong—he was already on his feet chasing her.

She knew she couldn't outrun him, so she changed course and threw herself into another cluster of plants. She needed to avoid engaging Peanut on the open floor, where he was most comfortable.

He plunged into the plants after her, thrashing his arms and legs to get past the stalks. Infinity turned around and landed a fist in the center of his face. He screeched in pain. She threw another jab and caught him in the mouth, turning the screech into a garbled grunt. She swung again, and again, gaining confidence with each punch.

The lemur freed his arms from the tangle and caught her right arm by the wrist. He yanked her fist to his mouth and bit down.

Infinity felt his teeth sink into her skin, and then heard her bones crack. The pain was overwhelming, but thanks to years of training and fighting she was able to overcome it and throw her left fist at the lemur's eye, landing a decent hit.

Peanut screeched again and released her fist.

She threw herself backward and tumbled out of the clump of plants. She hit the floor hard and skidded several feet on her butt. Instinctively, she rolled to her right and tried to push herself to her feet with her right hand. She collapsed immediately from the pain.

Plant stalks clattered as Peanut emerged from the cluster after her. Infinity rolled to her left, pushed herself to her feet, and took off running. The closest plant cluster was at least thirty yards away.

At twenty yards out, Infinity felt Peanut's hands grab her ankles, and she went down. Her right hand hit the floor so hard that the pain actually blinded her for a moment. By the time she could see again, the lemur was on top of her with his knees on either side of her neck and his feet locked together. He immediately applied crushing pressure. His legs were unbelievably strong. She tried kicking upward to clamp her legs around his neck, but he had already immobilized her legs with his arms.

Infinity twisted her neck, moving her throat out from under the pressure of the lemur's knees, but this left him pressing on both her carotid arteries, and her vision was starting to blur.

She somehow freed her left hand and jabbed it into the

creature's ribs. This was the most vulnerable spot she could reach, so she pulled back and jabbed again. Peanut grunted but didn't let up on her neck.

Infinity blinked. She could no longer see out of her right eye, and her head was starting to tingle. She drew back and drove her fist into Peanut's ribs again, and then again.

The lemur squirmed, obviously trying to escape the pain from her jabs.

Her left eye was now fading to black. She'd be out within seconds. She grunted, summoning every bit of strength she had, and rammed her fist into his ribs again.

This time he gasped, and his knees let up for a brief moment.

Infinity sprung into action, contracting her abdominal muscles and curling her body. She was able to slide her neck out from between the lemur's knees and toward his crotch. She redoubled this effort and continued folding herself until her face was inches from the peanut-sized bulge in his bodysuit. Infinity didn't hesitate—she clamped her teeth onto the bulge and began shaking her head.

The pressure from Peanut's legs quickly loosened as he panicked. Infinity took full advantage of the range of motion this offered, yanking her head viciously from side to side until her teeth tore through the lemur's bodysuit and blood flowed into her mouth.

Peanut scooted himself back and began pounding her legs with his fists.

Infinity shook her head one more time, nearly severing the bulge from the lemur's body. She then released it and got to her feet. The arena was strangely silent for a few moments as she stood gazing at her broken hand and Peanut curled up on his side, inspecting his own substantial damage. Infinity's fury then took over—she stepped forward on her left foot and stomped on the lemur's skull with her right, driving his head into the floor with devastating force.

The blow should have cracked his skull, but instead his head had sunk into the floor several inches and remained largely uninjured. The floor had softened at the exact moment of impact.

She stared down at the lemur, seething over his unfair advantage while he writhed with his hands cupped over his groin. Maybe she could pummel him to death the way Terry had killed his hunter, but this would be difficult without the use of her right hand. She'd have to use her feet.

She raised her foot to kick him again, but Peanut rolled away just before she brought it down. Growling with fury, he jumped to his feet and started coming at her.

"Goddammit!" she screamed. She took off running again.

16

———

TRADE

APRIL 11 - 9:10 PM

DESMOND TURNED AWAY from the screen. There was nothing he could do to help Infinity, and watching her ordeal made it impossible to think clearly.

He had already tried a half dozen ideas, all of which had gotten him nowhere. He had tried promising to take the city dwellers to an island on their own world that was populated by humans. The female lemur had dismissed this immediately, stating that she knew this to be false because her species already knew of every island on the planet. He had then offered to teach the city dwellers everything he knew as a biologist. She had dismissed this also. He had tried arguing that the city dwellers would be better off hunting non-sentient creatures. She'd replied that there would be no honor or fun in such hunts. He had taken Infinity's suggestion of trying to shame them by accusing them of cheating by giving Peanut an advantage. The lemur had ignored this attempt completely.

"Get him, Infinity!" Vic cried.

Desmond couldn't help but turn back to the screen. Infinity was now on her feet, and Peanut was curled up on the ground, bleeding profusely from his groin. Infinity delivered a vicious kick to his head, but he somehow recovered immediately, got to his feet, and started chasing her down. She'd have to turn and fight again soon, and her exhaustion was starting to show.

Infinity had given Desmond as much time as she could, and he'd gotten nowhere.

On the screen, Infinity turned and saw that she was about to be overtaken. She cut sharply to her left and ran full speed into a cluster of trees, allowing her impact with the plants to bring her to a stop. Desmond saw her face turn pale when her injured hand hit the plant stalks. She was in extreme pain.

Seconds later, Peanut slammed into the cluster. Infinity began swinging and kicking, blocking his attempts to grab hold of her again. She pulled a stalk from the floor and swung it at him, but this seemed to have little effect.

Infinity was running out of time.

Desmond rubbed his eyes furiously, trying to think. He tapped the camera lens in his forehead. "Kitty, I know you can hear me. If you bridge me back, even for just a few seconds, these lemurs will be convinced I have control over the bridging process. Then they'll listen to me. They'll make a deal. Please! Do it now."

Nothing.

He pounded his forehead in frustration. He only had one idea left that he hadn't tried. It was a desperate idea—something he should have never even considered in the first place. But he no longer cared now. Besides, it probably wouldn't work anyway.

"Okay, Kitty, how about this. I want to give the lemurs the

plans for building a bridging device—the Outlanders' instructions. If you bridge me back, I'll figure out a way to get the instructions, and I'll bridge back here. I'll give the instructions to the city dwellers. This is what you want us to do, isn't it?"

Desmond glanced at the lemurs in the room, but they were gone. The whole room was gone. He staggered and fell to his knees on the padded floor of the bridging chamber. He looked around—he was alone in the chamber.

Had he solved the puzzle, or was this just one of Kitty's tricks? He had no time to contemplate the implications. He got to his feet. "Armando? Hey! Anyone here?"

He heard a thump and then a hiss of air behind him. He turned in time to see the airlock hatch opening. A woman appeared in the doorway. Her face was vaguely familiar. Desmond remembered having met her the previous day, but that seemed so long ago. She was one of the med techs, Trini Soloman. "Trini?"

She leaned back out of the hatch. "Dr. Fornas? Mr. Doyle? You'd better get in here."

Desmond didn't wait. He went to the airlock and squeezed past Trini.

Armando and Fornas were approaching from the other side of the lab, both of them looking alarmed.

"Desmond, what happened?" Armando said as he glanced into the bridging chamber. "Where are the others? Where's Infinity?"

"Listen to me carefully," said Desmond. "The trial isn't over yet, and it hasn't been going well. We've suffered losses. But Infinity, Vic, and Terry are still alive." He grabbed Armando's shoulders and looked him directly in the eyes. "I came back here to save Infinity's life, and save this entire world in the process."

"How?" Armando asked, his voice unsteady.

"I don't have time to explain details, so I'm asking you to trust me. There are intelligent beings on the world we bridged to. I've come back to get the original data from the Outlanders' signal—the instructions for building a bridging device. I need to take it with me to give to those beings."

Armando and Fornas stared at him, apparently at a loss for words.

"It will save Infinity's life! And it's what Kitty wants us to do." Desmond was certain the first part of this was true, assuming Infinity was still alive. As for the second part, he was horrified that he could so blatantly claim this to be true without being certain. Billions of lives were at stake, and he hadn't even flinched as he'd said it.

Dr. Fornas furrowed his brows and mouthed something silently before speaking aloud. "But this is the reason our world is on trial in the first place. We can't give away the key to bridging—"

"Not the key," Desmond interjected. "Only the original instructions. These beings won't be able to figure out the key hidden within the instructions. Please, we have to hurry."

"Desmond," Armando said, "are you saying you want to destroy that world? The world you just told us is populated by intelligent beings?"

"I don't have time to explain it all! Please, I need to know —is it even possible to convert the data from the Outlanders' signal into a form that will bridge back with me?"

Again the two men stared. After several seconds, Fornas said, "We have tried to prepare for all possible scenarios. Yes, we do have several copies of the entire data set imprinted on organic fabric. Just as we have copies of the key."

Desmond felt a small seed of hope forming. "I don't want

the key, only the data from the original signal. Can you get it for me right now?"

Fornas pursed his lips and shook his head. "What you're asking is... of grave import, to put it mildly. Colonel Chislett arrived this afternoon and has assumed authority over all decisions concerning—"

Desmond glanced around. "It doesn't look like Colonel Chislett is here at the moment, and time is not on our side. Tell me the truth—if we get the colonel involved, how long do you think it will be before I can get what I need and bridge back?"

Both men shook their heads, obviously having the same opinion of Colonel Chislett. "It would never happen," Fornas said.

"Look," Desmond said, "I really, *honestly* believe this is the decision Kitty and her species will judge us on. They want to know, do we have the ability—the decisiveness—to carry out the mission they believe in? They believe the ultimate mission is to eliminate entire civilizations based on how they use bridging technology. I'm going to show them we have this ability."

Again, precious seconds of silence.

"Why not just give this civilization the coordinates of the Outlanders' signal?" Armando asked.

Desmond took a deep breath to avoid shouting in frustration. "The universe diverged from ours at least forty million years ago. There's almost no chance the Outlanders existed at all in that timeline."

Armando turned to Fornas. "I believe him, Kyle. This world is my home, too, and I think we should give him the data. If he says we can't wait for the colonel, we can't wait."

Fornas raised a trembling hand to his forehead and whispered, "Holy Mary, mother of God." He then turned and rushed away.

Desmond glanced at Trini. The med tech was standing within earshot. She was staring at him, her eyes wide and her mouth half open. Desmond turned to Armando.

"Save Infinity," Armando said softly. "Please."

Anyone else would have seen this as an odd request, considering the enormity of what was at stake, but Desmond understood perfectly, and he suddenly felt less alone.

Fornas came hustling back, carrying a black tube. His hand was still shaking as he handed it to Desmond. "It's printed in a binary code that any reasonably-intelligent beings should be able to—"

Desmond snatched the tube and tucked it under his shirt, hoping this might ensure that it would bridge back with him. He tapped the camera in his forehead. "Okay, Kitty, I've got it, and I'm ready to come back!"

Nothing happened.

Armando said, "How could you possibly communicate with her if she's in the other timeline?"

Desmond started to shake his head, but then he dropped a fraction of an inch to the floor and had to wobble slightly to keep his balance. He was back in the viewing room with Vic and Terry. He spun around and studied the video screen.

Infinity was there, still alive. She was cupping her injured right hand in her left and was now limping, with a bloody bite or cut visible on her left thigh. Now she was alone. No, actually she wasn't alone. Desmond spotted Peanut, following her a few dozen yards back. He was obviously hurt, too, and was leaving a thick trail of blood on the floor. He was holding a hand over one eye and was shaking his head violently every few seconds as if he had some kind of nerve damage.

Desmond took a moment to breathe. She was still alive. He stared at the screen, processing this fact and trying not to let his emotions overwhelm him. Finally, he pulled his eyes from the screen and turned around. There were now eight city dwellers in the room, all of them staring at him.

Desmond had momentarily forgotten about the tube he'd been carrying. He tightened his grip on it, relieved that it was still there, and pulled it from beneath his shirt. "I have just bridged to my own world and back," he said to the lemurs. "You watched it happen, so you cannot deny that I have the ability to bridge."

He waited for his translator to catch up and then continued. "If you could bridge to other worlds like I can, you would have access to countless other intelligent species. You could hunt and kill them. Or maybe you could even learn from them. But you'll never be able to bridge to other worlds without the instructions for building a bridging device."

After the translation ended, he held up the tube. "I have those instructions right here. If you stop the hunt right now and agree to let us all live, I will give you the instructions. You should trust me when I say these instructions will change your civilization forever."

"What the hell, Desmond!" Vic shouted. "We ain't giving them nothing! It ain't—"

Vic vanished.

"Oh Jesus," Terry said as he stared at the spot where his fellow Marine had been only seconds before. "Desmond, what's going on?"

Desmond suddenly felt confident that he was doing exactly what Kitty wanted. Vic had tried to interfere, and she had promptly bridged him out of the room—hopefully to a safe place and not to his death.

Desmond ignored Terry and continued addressing the

lemurs. "You see? You see what we are capable of?" He shook the tube above his head. "Stop the hunt now!"

The lemurs looked at each other and began exchanging what sounded like heated comments.

Desmond glanced back at the screen. Infinity was still limping, moving as fast as her injuries would allow. But Peanut was right behind her. His head was twitching less, and he seemed to be moving faster now. He would overtake her in seconds.

"Stop the hunt right now!" Desmond cried. "Or I'll bridge out of here with these instructions, and you'll never see them again."

The female lemur emitted a series of shrill barks and whistles. Desmond's translator remained silent—she wasn't speaking to him. She pointed at the screen.

Desmond turned. Peanut was no more than five feet behind Infinity. He would throw himself forward and tackle her at any moment.

But then Peanut abruptly stopped. He tilted his head slightly as if listening to something. After several seconds, he took a long look at Infinity. She was still moving, quickly increasing the distance between them. The lemur then ducked clumsily into a fighting stance, wobbling a few times before finding his balance. The video cut to Infinity, and the lemur voices narrating the fight over the video feed began speaking more rapidly, obviously agitated.

The female lemur approached Desmond and began speaking. His translator interpreted. "If the words you speak are true, then we will not hunt and kill you, and we will give you wealth. If the words you speak are not true, then our wealthiest and most honorable hunters will hunt and kill you in the arena. Know that my words are true."

Desmond said, "I'm telling the truth. I promise." He then handed her the tube.

The female lemur and the room around her vanished, replaced by the white interior of the bridging chamber. A split-second later the black tube appeared inches from Desmond's outstretched hand and fell to the floor. He heard Infinity grunt a few feet to his left and turned in time to see her collapse, smearing blood onto the smooth, white floor.

Desmond dropped to his knees. "Infinity!" He lifted her to a sitting position and then pulled her into a hug.

She grunted in pain and said, "Watch the hand!" Then she threw her left arm around him and held on fiercely.

Vic spoke up from behind Desmond. "You need to explain, and it better be good."

Desmond loosened his hold on Infinity and turned around.

Vic was sitting cross-legged by the wall. To his left, Terry was pushing himself up onto his butt.

"Vic," said Desmond, "I'm sorry, I...." He trailed off when he noticed a prone figure beside Terry. It was Gideon. The guardsman was pale from blood loss. His shoulder was badly mangled, but the wound appeared to have been cleaned and cared for.

Gideon struggled to crane his neck until he could see the others in the chamber. "Goddamn, you all are a sight for sore eyes. But I think bridging back robbed me of my bandages and stitches. I need to be sewn up again."

"We need med techs in here!" Desmond shouted.

The hatch popped open, and techs rushed in, followed by Armando and Fornas.

Vic spoke up again over the commotion. "Desmond, you need to explain. We all deserve an explanation."

"Yes," said Dr. Fornas, "please explain what's going on."

Desmond turned to Infinity, who was still in his arms. Her eyes were searching his.

"What happened?" she asked.

He sucked in a deep breath. "I don't really know for sure. Not yet."

17

MIGRANTS

APRIL 11 - 10:00 PM

INFINITY WAITED for Desmond to explain what had happened, but he just stared at her, slightly shaking his head. The skin around his eyes was taut—he was deeply troubled.

She squeezed his shoulder with her left hand. "What happened, partner?"

He bent down and picked up a two-foot-long black tube. He pried the cap off one end and looked inside. "It came back with me. Kitty didn't let them keep it."

Infinity eyed the tube. "What is that?"

"It's the Outlanders' instructions," he said. "I was going to give it to the lemurs. I *did* give it to them." One of his eyes twitched almost imperceptibly.

"Why'd they bridge us back?" Vic asked. "Did your little stunt make us fail the test?"

Desmond eyes flitted nervously toward the Marine. "I

don't know. I hope not. It was the only thing I could think of that I hadn't already tried. And Infinity was... I don't know."

"What's going to happen now?" Dr. Fornas asked, his voice hinting at panic.

A slight change in air pressure tickled Infinity's ears. Something appeared to her left and she turned. It was Kitty's mechanical pod. The machine was gleaming and clean, despite having been buried in the dirt for over twenty-four hours.

Kitty gazed at the humans through the pod's portals for a moment and then opened its hatch. She pulled herself out and then started what appeared to be a stretching routine, touching the floor, extending her arms toward the chamber ceiling, and rubbing her butt muscles. If not for the ornately-dyed fur covering her entire body, Kitty would've looked almost human while doing this. Infinity noticed the woman still smelled like flowers, despite having been confined to the tiny pod for so long.

Kitty held her translator to her mouth and spoke softly in her rapid-fire language. The translator interpreted in near-perfect English. "We will not give you consequences for violating our rules."

Everyone in the chamber remained silent, waiting for an explanation.

When it became clear Kitty wasn't going to elaborate, Desmond spoke up. "I was going to give the Outlanders' instructions to the lemurs, without the key. I decided maybe that's what you wanted us to do."

Kitty listened to her translator and then spoke. "Yes, and we will not give you consequences."

"We lost eleven men," Vic said. "They were good men— friends of mine."

Again, Kitty listened and then spoke. "Yes. But now you will not have consequences."

"So you're not going to destroy our world?" Fornas asked.

"No."

Someone tapped Infinity's shoulder. She turned, and a med tech handed her a paper gown. Infinity had forgotten she was naked. She nodded to the tech and accepted the gown.

The tech gently took Infinity's right wrist and examined her broken hand. "This is serious, hon. And that looks like a nasty bite on your thigh. Why don't you come with me to the lab."

Infinity pulled her hand back. "Soon."

Desmond spoke to Kitty. "What will happen to the lemurs and their world?"

"They will not be able to build a bridging device because we did not allow them to keep the Outlanders' instructions. Your intent was important. The act was not."

Desmond shuffled his feet awkwardly. "I'm glad you didn't, but why didn't you allow them to keep the instructions?"

Kitty tilted her head to the side in a strange gesture. "Perhaps we will eventually allow the lemurs to keep the instructions. But for now the lemur world is useful to us. It is a suitable world for conducting trials, such as the trial you have just completed."

"I was going to give it to them," Desmond said.

"Yes, you intended to. But you had no intention of giving them the key to bridging technology. This is what we wished to know about you. Now we know that you understand the Outlanders' purpose. The Outlanders' purpose is important and wise and foremost. Some civilizations can be allowed to exist. Other civilizations should not be allowed to exist. You were willing to destroy the lemurs' civilization by giving them the Outlanders' instructions. Now we know you understand the Outlanders' purpose."

"You could have just fucking asked us," said Terry, who was still sitting on the floor.

Kitty listened to her translator and then smiled at Terry. "We have done trials such as this many times before. Words are often not true. Actions are more often true."

Dr. Fornas cleared his throat. "If I may be so bold, can we now expect that you'll remove those green cone devices from outside our facility?"

Kitty smiled again. "They have already been removed."

Fornas clapped his hands together. "Thank the heavens!"

Kitty listened to her translator, and then her smile faded slightly. She fired off a long, bewildering string of rapid speech. Her translator began responding while she was still speaking. "This is a turning point for your civilization. You may choose to destroy your bridging device. Other civilizations have done so when faced with similar turning points. However, these civilizations typically do not progress very far beyond the state they were in when they decided to destroy their bridging devices. Alternatively, if you do not destroy your bridging device, and you continue to learn from bridging technology, your civilization may flourish beyond anything you can imagine. As you know, the key to bridging technology was purposefully hidden within the Outlanders' instructions. What you do not know is that the key to bridging technology is only the first level of hidden information in these instructions. There are deeper levels, each requiring progressively greater intelligence and skill to understand. Of course, if you choose to continue using your bridging device, we will monitor your progress and ensure that you do not violate the rules. As you know, there must be consequences for violating rules."

Kitty waited for the translation to end before making one last comment. "As I said, this is a turning point for your civilization."

Infinity glanced at Fornas. His expression had lost all signs of fear. In fact, he was grinning, and Infinity sensed he was practically drooling over the thought of being a part of his civilization's turning point. But Infinity felt no such excitement. She'd had enough. Bridging brought nothing but destruction and misery. There was no chance in hell Fornas and his people would destroy their bridging center. They would continue bridging, exploring new worlds, and exposing their entire civilization to new threats. Kitty and her species would forever be monitoring them, ready to inflict consequences at the slightest violation of rules. Infinity would inevitably get sucked back into the whole process. Once a bridger, always a bridger. She turned to Desmond. He looked back at her, frowning, and somehow she knew he was thinking the same thing.

She turned to speak to Kitty, but Desmond beat her to it. "I have a question," he said. "Is there any way that a small group of us could get away from all this? Is there any version of Earth at all, in any universe, where we wouldn't have to worry about being watched or being destroyed simply because someone has made a mistake?"

Kitty listened intently as her device translated. She then smiled even more broadly than before. "I am pleased by your question, Desmond. In fact, we were hoping you would ask this question. Yes, such an arrangement is possible."

Infinity waited for more, but Kitty just kept smiling. "How?" Infinity asked. "How can there be a version of Earth that can't be destroyed?"

Kitty replied, "We have designated many such worlds. We can say with certainty that they will not be destroyed because we do not allow bridging to these worlds. Only we can bridge to these worlds. We are hoping to bridge Desmond and others like him to one of these worlds. In fact, this is one of the reasons I have returned here following your trial. You and Desmond, and the others of your team, have shown us that you understand the Outlanders' purpose, as well as having other qualities we value. We are pleased that we will not have to give you consequences. We are hoping to bridge Desmond and others like him to one of the worlds we have designated. Desmond and his friends may then populate the world, which would please us. Subsequent bridging to the world would never be allowed. Destroying the world would never be allowed. Desmond and his friends, and then their children, and the children of their children, will never be disturbed or destroyed. This would please us very much."

Infinity chewed her lower lip, considering Kitty's words. Something about Kitty's proposal made her uneasy. Desmond started to say something, but Infinity cut him off. "I'm Desmond's partner. I go where he goes. But I can't have children. So I guess that's a deal-breaker."

Kitty frowned. "Why can't you have children?"

This question caught Infinity off guard. After hesitating briefly, she put a hand on her abdomen. "I was injured when I was sixteen. Stabbed right here with a knife. Three times."

Kitty listened to her translator and replied without hesitating. "Such physical damage can be repaired easily. I have the proper tools and would be happy to do it myself if you would like me to."

A sensation of weightlessness overtook Infinity's arms and spread up to her scalp. "Are you serious?"

"Yes, I am serious," Kitty replied. "The damage will be

easy to repair. It is not a deal-breaker. I could repair the damage now if you wish. My pod is equipped with the proper tools."

Infinity turned to Desmond. She wasn't sure what to say, or if there was anything to say at all. He extended his hand, palm up. She put her left hand into his, and he squeezed gently. For just a moment, she allowed herself to believe what Kitty had said. But then the moment ended.

She shook her head and turned back to Kitty. "Yesterday I watched you murder a pregnant lemur, a sentient being. Why would you be interested in repairing my damage?"

"My action yesterday was needed in order to stimulate your conflict with the city-dwelling lemurs. My offer to repair your damage today is needed to enable you and Desmond to help populate the world you wish to inhabit. Different needs require different actions."

Desmond said, "Okay, so forgive me for being skeptical, but this all sounds too good to be true. There's a catch, right? What do we have to do in return?"

Kitty renewed her smile as she listened to the translation. "What we ask in return is that you thrive and find happiness and populate the world. I must also tell you that another sentient species will exist on the destination world. They are peaceful and will not be a danger to you. They are a remarkable species. But they are somewhat unique in that they thrive only when they are able to interact with another sentient species."

Infinity felt her weightlessness begin to dissolve. So there *was* a catch. "You want to send us there for the benefit of this other species? I suppose they will hunt and kill us for honor? Or are we to be their food source? Or perhaps their slaves?"

Kitty replied, "You are suspicious. But this species is peaceful and will not be a danger to you, I assure you. You will benefit from their presence, and they will benefit from yours. They are on each of the worlds we have chosen, and for the same reasons that are important to you—they wish to live simply and without fear, to thrive, and to be happy. No civilization, not even my own, will ever bridge to any of these worlds or destroy any of these worlds. The worlds we have chosen are suitable to your biological needs, and your options are diverse. You may choose a world that has the environmental conditions you prefer."

Infinity glanced around the room. The others were silent, listening to the conversation. Her eyes met Desmond's. He simply raised his brows at her.

She turned back to Kitty. "I'm not saying that we're agreeing to this yet, but I *have* always wanted to live by a beach."

May 2 - 5:49 AM - 21 days later

"Looks like a lot has changed here in twenty-one years," Infinity said.

She and Desmond had been unable to sleep, so they had borrowed a car and driven to West Plains. This was their first venture outside the National Bridging Center, and it would be their last chance to spend a few hours on their own. In spite of the darkness, they wanted to take a look at this world, which had diverged from theirs twenty years before Armando's group had bridged here nineteen months ago. Neither of them had ever been to West Plains—it was simply the closest town.

The two were now sitting atop a picnic table in a park,

Infinity leaning back against Desmond's chest. This positioning of their bodies had a special meaning for both of them, having been the way they'd spent their first night together, hiding from killer birds in a tree. A few yards to their right was a bronze plaque explaining why the park's name had been changed from People's Park to Freeborn Park. Apparently, a doctor named Linus Freeborn had established a quarantine facility in his local clinic at the height of the red howler fever epidemic fifteen years ago, saving hundreds of lives and paying the price with his own. After parking the car at the park, Infinity and Desmond had taken a walk through the darkened town. With the help of street lamps, they had seen lingering evidence of the epidemic's severity: burned buildings that had been abandoned to rot, warning signs still affixed to stores and houses that had long been vacant, and rusting sections of tall fencing.

Desmond rested his chin on her shoulder. "Yeah. And then my actions nearly destroyed what's left of this world."

She turned her head and gave him a bite on his chin. "This world is still here *because* of what you did. You saved these people. You need to accept that and get over it."

He remained silent for several seconds. Then he said, "The ring-tails were decent beings. So were the white lemurs. I'm guessing the species in the other enclosures were decent as well. But I was willing to let their world implode the way ours did—willing to kill them all. That's not something you just get over."

Infinity groaned. They had gone over this more than enough times. "Kitty didn't allow it to happen. That's it. Done. And even if she had, those species probably would have been better off dead anyway. You were under extreme pressure, and you came up with a brilliant strategy—and it turned out to be the right strategy. You know how I look at it? My man is willing to do anything to keep me safe. *Anything*. How many women can make that claim and know with complete certainty that it's true?"

His chest heaved as he sighed. He then put his arm around her, slipped it under her t-shirt, and stroked the three old scars on her belly.

She placed her right hand on his and guided his fingers to the new scar, from a puncture only three millimeters wide. Kitty's work had been quick and painless.

"How's the hand?" he asked, brushing her ear with his lips.

She flexed her fingers. "Still tender. Full motion is almost back." She put her hand back on his as he drew circles around her tiny scar.

After perhaps a full minute of silence, she said, "Tell me something—if I were gone, and you met Passerina, do you think you two would hit it off?" She was referring to Passerina Stroud, the other version of herself who had always lived on this world. Passerina had flown to Missouri over a week ago to spend the day with Infinity and Desmond.

Desmond stiffened a little. "Are you serious?"

She waited silently.

"I have a feeling there's no correct answer," he said. "Yes, she's incredible because she's you. But no, she's also not my type because she isn't really you. How's that?"

She hit the back of her head against his chest. "It's a pussy answer."

They both fell silent and stared at the eastern sky, which was starting to turn orange. Infinity's thoughts continued to dwell on the other version of herself. Passerina had decided not to bring her son, Maslin. She'd left him at home with her husband in Phoenix. Perhaps this was for the best—the thought of meeting Maslin, and then having to tell him goodbye forever, terrified Infinity.

"Just a few minutes until sunrise," Desmond said. "Less than two hours till we bridge out. It took fifty minutes to drive here."

Infinity scanned the surrounding area. It was still fairly dark, and the park was completely empty. Perfect.

Desmond must have been thinking the same thing because his hand started sliding downward past her scars. "It's our last opportunity on this world," he whispered.

She arched her back slightly. "Then I guess we'd better make it really memorable."

MAY 2 - 7:51 AM

WHITE, weatherproof boxes of various sizes were stacked from floor to ceiling in the bridging chamber, filling almost half the room. A cargo net was stretched over the boxes to prevent them from tumbling when they bridged. Twenty-two migrants and a handful of techs filled the other half of the chamber. Infinity grabbed the nearest tech's wrist and looked at his watch. Nine minutes to bridge-out—far too long to stand around smelling sweat and listening to nervous chatter. She gave Desmond a look and then stepped through the airlock into the lab.

Desmond followed her out, as did Armando, Lenny, and Xavier.

"You can't change your mind now, Infinity," said Lenny. "It took two freaking weeks to gather all this crap."

Infinity just shook her head. She and the other migrants had spent the last two weeks filling the boxes in the bridging chamber with all the camping and survival supplies they'd been able to procure. They'd gotten most of the stuff as donations from stores looking for a bit of positive publicity. The government had been reluctant to get involved in this endeavor, probably afraid of doing anything that might anger Kitty and her people. So most of the gear and supplies were consumer quality rather than military grade. Kitty had assured Infinity's team that anything they could fit in the chamber would bridge with them, regardless of whether it consisted of living tissue. Apparently this was one of the capabilities that could only be accessed by decrypting one of the deeper layers of data in the Outlanders' instructions.

Infinity gazed at Armando. The poor guy was sweating profusely. "You sure you're up for this?" she asked.

He tried to smile. "I'm not losing you and Desmond—not again. I'm sticking with you until you've made me a grandfather."

Armando wasn't actually Infinity's father, but he was the closest thing she had. And she was the closest thing he had to a daughter.

"We're sticking with you too," Lenny said, slapping Infinity and Desmond on their backs. "Isabelle and I wouldn't miss out on this for nothin'. Daisy's just a pup, but she's a seasoned explorer of worlds."

Daisy was indeed only eleven months old. She was currently the only child in Infinity's close-knit family, although Xavier and Celia were expecting within two months. Reece Eagleton and Chloe Hunt were also expecting, within two weeks, in fact, but they had decided to remain on this world so that Chloe could give birth in a real hospital. Infinity could hardly blame them for that.

"Celia and I are with you too, Des," Xavier added. "For better or worse."

Desmond leaned back toward the chamber and peered inside. "Not much of a colony, but we'll make it work. We've done it before, right?"

Infinity followed his gaze, assessing the other migrants. All the surviving members of her family from the arthropod world except for Reece and Chloe had decided to stay together, in spite of the possible risks. Including Gideon. Thanks to some medical help from Kitty, the guardsman hadn't lost his arm, and his shoulder was healing. The Marine Vic Shepherd had also volunteered, and he had actually convinced his girlfriend to come with him. The other surviving Marine, Terry, had decided he never wanted to see another alternate world and was staying here.

That was it—seventeen migrants. At least it had been until four days ago, when five strangers had been added to the roster without explanation. Colonel Camron Chislett had apparently recruited them. Four women and one man, all of them about thirty years old. Infinity and Desmond had requested to interview them, and had been granted permission, but they'd been told that they had little say in the final selection of migrants. About all they'd been able to determine was that the newcomers had seen news reports about the colony of migrants and wanted to be part of it. They appeared to be physically fit, and they had all said that they were reproductively viable, as far as they knew. Infinity decided she might as well welcome these new volunteers, considering no other people from this world were interested in abandoning their home world, which they perceived to be safe. She only hoped that they fully understood what they were getting themselves into.

Infinity was getting bored with waiting. She examined her

right hand, flexing her fingers. Not only had Kitty's medical skills and technology saved Gideon's arm, but she had also accelerated the healing of Infinity's broken hand. Kitty had performed another procedure, of course, intended to repair the damage from Infinity's old knife wounds. But in recent weeks Infinity had been working on forcing herself to stop dwelling on this, because she had no idea whether she'd ever find out if it had been successful.

One of the techs poked her head out of the airlock. "Three minutes, folks."

Infinity inhaled deeply and then felt herself fighting back a smile. She should have been terrified. What if Kitty's promises of safety and peace had been lies? But she was still tingling from her experience on the picnic table in West Plains. She was also adrenalized, anticipating what was to come. Not because she was about to bridge—she was done with bridging—but because this time it really would be her *last* bridge.

She took Desmond's hand, and the two of them led the way back into the bridging chamber, Armando, Lenny, and Xavier following close behind. The techs exited without saying much of anything, and the airlock hatch closed behind them.

The twenty-two migrants stood there awkwardly, waiting.

"Are they supposed to come here and help us with this, or what?" Xavier asked.

Infinity shook her head. "Kitty assured me that it would simply happen. At eight o'clock." She turned and looked at the faces around her. "Normally, I'd give advice on how to deal with the bridging process, but I'm pretty sure my old spiel would be useless now. Bridging these days isn't anything like—"

Infinity fell silent. She squinted against the brightness of the morning sun. A breeze tickled the three weeks worth of stubble on her scalp and fluttered through the fabric of her t-shirt and shorts. She felt Desmond's hand grasp hers.

Daisy let out a delighted giggle.

"I'll be damned," said Hayley Millwright, one of the members of Infinity's original colony and former President of the United States. "It's true. Everything Kitty told us is true!"

Infinity turned slowly, taking in the scene. The supply boxes were sitting beside the migrants, still neatly stacked, though they were now resting upon a wide stretch of golden sand. Beyond the sand was forest, gradually rising up a low hill, with a taller hill in the distance behind it.

She kept turning. No more than a hundred yards from where she was standing, waves of greenish water were washing up onto the beach and then gradually withdrawing, leaving a wide expanse of wet sand that sparkled in the sunlight like stars in the night sky. A short distance out from the shore, the water faded to sky blue, with multicolored patches of coral reef visible below the surface. A mile or so offshore was another strip of beach lined by another forest—an island. To the right of that, and to the left, and beyond it as far as Infinity could see were more islands, all of them covered in pristine forest with no signs of any kind of civilization.

She squeezed Desmond's hand. "It really is true," she whispered.

Desmond pointed. "Look at that, Infinity!"

A massive creature, at least the size of a whale, was breaching a few hundred yards offshore. Its arched back cut through the surface, with numerous evenly-spaced ridges along its length.

"It's beautiful," someone exclaimed.

Infinity squinted, and then she drew in a sharp breath.

Something about the ridges didn't look quite right. Just as the creature's back went under, its tail emerged and hovered above the surface for a moment before slipping out of view again. Now Infinity was certain of it. The thing wasn't a creature at all—it was a machine.

Bridgers 6: The Bond of Absolution

On the brink of extinction, a final struggle begins.

Earth is dead. Infinity and Desmond, the only surviving bridgers, believe they've been given one final chance to find peace. Leading a small group of migrants, they bridge to a new world for the last time.

Their new home appears to be perfect—pristine islands encircled by sparkling beaches and a coral sea. However, there is one catch—they're not alone.

Infinity, Desmond, and their fellow migrants knew they'd have to share their new home with another sentient species. They were told these other beings would not be a threat. Soon, however, they discover another camp like their own. Except this camp's occupants have all been slaughtered.

The human colonists have been deceived. The resident sentient beings are not so benign, and this world isn't safe. But when the real danger becomes apparent, it's not what anyone expected.

AUTHOR'S NOTES

Some of you may have questions. So I have decided to offer my thoughts on a few things related to **Bridgers 5: The Trial of Extinction**. These topics are in no particular order, and they may not even be important to most people. But if you are at all interested, here you go.

Is it really possible that lemurs could have evolved to be this intelligent? Yes, it's possible, although perhaps not very likely. But when you have infinite do-overs of Earth's history, the unlikely becomes much more likely. The appearance of intelligent lemurs is certainly more likely than the appearance of intelligent mosquitoes or salamanders. Lemurs, after all, are primates. They have hands with dexterous fingers. They also have thumbs, although their thumbs are not truly opposable (they are called pseudo-opposable thumbs). Let's consider the hypothetical scenarios proposed by Infinity and Desmond in **Bridgers 5**. Desmond suggests that, if the monkeys and apes (simians) had never appeared on Earth, the prosimians (lemurs, tarsiers, lorises) and others would have had a much better chance of diversifying. Monkeys are particularly competitive and aggressive, and it would be extremely difficult for other species to outcompete them in their habitat. But if some random event had prevented the simians from evolving, the prosimians (and perhaps other types of primates) likely would have diversified, and our world would be filled with numerous new creatures. It is possible that one of those could have evolved human-like intelligence. Again, maybe not likely, but certainly possible.

Infinity then suggests that perhaps lemurs evolved to be highly intelligent while they were isolated on Madagascar, and after becoming intelligent, they spread out from that island and eventually displaced (or intentionally killed) the monkeys and apes. This didn't happen on our version of Earth, but perhaps on another version—another timeline— some random event (like a change in climate or the immigration of some species into Madagascar that forced the lemurs to adapt in a different way) could have resulted in environmental pressure on the lemurs that makes it more advantageous for them to develop problem-solving skills and reasoning ability.

Is it really possible there could be nine different sentient, intelligent species on one world? This is not only possible, it has happened on our version of Earth. Until very recently, humans shared this planet with others intelligent species. About 30,000 years ago, in addition to our species, there were at least three other hominin species that existed at the same time: the *Neanderthals* in Europe and western Asia, the *Denisovans* in Asia, and the *"hobbits"* from the Indonesian island of Flores. The question of why *Homo sapiens* is the only surviving species is a fascinating one, which does not yet have a definite answer. By the way, the "hominins" are a group of hominids that includes the genus *Homo* (humans, including our species and others) but excludes the gorillas, chimps, and orangutans. There are at least eight different "human" species (in the genus *Homo*) that we know of. As you can probably imagine, even more species have probably existed that we have not yet discovered. The world described in **Bridgers 5** has nine species of lemurs that have evolved language and human-like intelligence. If we can assume that lemurs could become intelligent, then we must assume it's possible for numerous intelligent species to exist at the same time.

What's up with these weird solid objects that suddenly turn soft? In the arena, Infinity (and Terry) are given a cutting tool that works just long enough for them to cut themselves free of their bindings, and then the tool mysteriously becomes soft ("like a slice of brown, melting cheese"). Also, Infinity tries using a "plant stalk" as a weapon, which doesn't go well. Yes, this is confusing, especially to Infinity and the other humans. Another thing that is confusing to them is how the lemurs can have walls and doorways that suddenly appear and disappear (including the massive walls in the arena). I suppose I took a risk of confounding the reader, but my intent was to show that the lemurs had discovered some way to remotely change the properties of a certain type of solid. Notice that this particular solid is always brown in color. Perhaps the solid objects have a tiny receiver embedded in them that can receive a wireless signal and then produce a certain frequency of vibration that temporarily makes the material soft, or perhaps even makes it turn from a solid to a gas (as with the walls). Anyway, I thought it would be fun to give the lemurs a few mysterious tech capabilities that baffle the humans. If you found this to be confusing, imagine how Infinity feels!

What have Infinity, Desmond, and their fellow colonists been eating during the last nineteen months? Many of the details of this are described in **Bridgers 4**. But it is important to point out that, on the "arthropod world," there was a variety of animals they could eat. In fact, they even figured out how to keep several of these in pens near Mossview (the framework mound they converted into a shelter). Although it wasn't specifically stated in **Bridgers 4**, we should assume that they experimented with eating various species of moss and aquatic algae in order to get some of the other nutrients they needed.

Why did the clothing, shoes, and weapons need to be made of living tissue? Because one of the limitations of bridging is that only living tissue can bridge (as well as some of the fluids and other elements inside of a living body). So, unless you want to arrive naked and weaponless on the destination world, you need to have clothing and weapons made of living tissue. These items were not available until Armando worked with the scientists on his new home world to develop them. I recently read a few articles about people growing articles of clothing from living human tissue (or tissue from other animals). So this is a very realist concept. The weapons are a bit more of a stretch of the imagination, but it isn't difficult to imagine that muscles and highly-elastic tendons could be configured to propel a dart at high velocity. I think it's possible, and the only reason we haven't created such weapons is that we've never had a real need for them.

How did Armando and the Marines bridge to the arthropod world? This is something that would have been impossible without the information contained within the "key" to bridging technology. If you'll remember, the mongrels gave this key (in the form of 900 symbols) to Desmond in **Bridgers 3**. The Outlanders concealed various keys within their instructions for building a bridging device, instructions that they transmitted through space by radio signal tens of thousands of years ago. The key the mongrels gave Desmond was really just the first of numerous keys within the Outlanders' signal. Each subsequent key requires a higher level of intelligence to discover and decrypt. The mongrels had only decrypted the first of these keys (and they paid dearly for giving it to Desmond). Anyway, this key allowed Armando, Dr. Fornas, and other scientists to add additional capabilities to their bridging device. One of these capabilities allowed them to identify all of the worlds (universes) to which humans have previously bridged. In this way, Armando was able to figure out which world Infinity's colony had bridged to nineteen months ago.

What's up with Kitty and the rest of her species? Kitty's species evolved on a different version of Earth. They are very human-like and would likely be classified in the genus *Homo*. They have fine black fur covering their bodies, and they have developed a language that is spoken very rapidly. They are far more advanced technologically than humans. It so happens that the Outlanders existed in Kitty's universe also, and Kitty's people discovered the Outlanders' signal long ago. It can be assumed that Kitty's people did not make the same mistake the humans on Infinity's Earth made—they did not destroy their world by using the lowest version of bridging devices (which, by design of the Outlanders, destroy the world of the beings who use them). Instead, Kitty's people were more cautious, and they discovered the "key" hidden within the instructions. This prompted them to look even more closely, and they eventually discovered the next deeper key. And perhaps they were smart enough to discover even deeper, more valuable keys.

Why did Kitty's people put humans on trial? It's important to understand that Kitty's people think highly of the Outlanders. In fact, you could even say they worship the Outlanders. They've never actually met the Outlanders, of course, because the Outlanders lived tens of thousands of years ago on a planet thousands of light years from Earth. Space travel to such a place is not possible, or at the very least, not practical. Nevertheless, Kitty's people revere the Outlanders. Their adoration of the Outlander civilization cannot be overstated. In fact, they have taken it upon themselves to forever enforce the rules that they believe are consistent with the Outlanders' mission. One of their rules is that the various encrypted "keys" to bridging technology should only be possessed by civilizations intelligent enough to discover them and figure out their meaning without assistance. The mongrels gave Desmond the key, thus violating this rule. Kitty's people destroyed all the worlds the mongrels had ever bridged to, and Kitty's people put the mongrels themselves on trial (we do not know how that trial ended). And since Desmond accepted the key from the mongrels, they put humans on trial. It's a rather high-stakes trial, with complete annihilation of Armando's new home world being the consequence of failure. This world also now happens to be the new home world of Infinity, Desmond, and the rest of their group (until the very end of **Bridgers 5**).

Did Kitty really spend 27 hours buried in the soil of the lemur world? Yep. After she initiated conflict between the humans and city dwellers in a really horrendous way (killing a pregnant lemur), she went into hiding. Her capsule is high-tech and produces plenty of fresh air for her to breathe (and is probably stocked with tasty snacks and drinks). From that safe hiding place, she could sit and watch the humans as they struggled to survive and to figure out how to prove that their world shouldn't be destroyed.

Why didn't the city dwellers keep their fences in good repair? Well, let's face it, the city-dwelling lemurs are like humans in some ways. They can build impressive cities, but they tend to neglect their poor and the infrastructure of various portions of their cities. They tend to be self-centered, and they only care about their current interests. The enclosure fences were mainly built to keep the poor city-dwelling lemurs (those living in the shantytowns) from getting into the enclosures to hunt the captive lemur species. Only the wealthy should have that privilege. Also, the fences were originally intended to keep the eight species of hunted lemurs contained. But after a period of time, it got to the point at which the hunted lemurs had nowhere to go if they escaped their enclosures. As strange as it sounds, the ring-tails (and the seven other hunted species) are better off inside their enclosures. At least only one of them is hunted per day there. They regularly sneak out of their enclosures to scavenge for items discarded by the city dwellers (they integrate these into the construction of their dwellings), but they never stay out for very long. In a world full of city dwellers that hope for the privilege of killing them, being outside the enclosure is not desirable.

What did Desmond do that actually caused Kitty to decide not to destroy the humans' home world? Desmond did the unthinkable—he gave the instructions to bridging technology to the city-dwelling lemurs, knowing full well that they would destroy their entire world by constructing and using bridging devices (because he only gave them the *instructions*, not the *key*). He did this as a last resort, in complete desperation. Partly because he wanted to prevent Infinity's death in the arena. That sounds monumentally selfish, doesn't it? I mean, he was willing to kill billions of intelligent lemurs, including the ring-tails, the innocent species that befriended him and his team. But... it is important to understand that Desmond also believed that this action was exactly what Kitty and her people were hoping for. This action was consistent with the Outlanders' mission—to eliminate civilizations incapable of deciphering the key hidden in the Outlanders' instructions. He believed this was the only way to pass their test. It was a big risk, but he decided to take it.

But wait! Desmond didn't know that Kitty wasn't going to allow him to actually hand over the Outlanders' instructions. So he was still willing to sacrifice this entire lemur world, right? That's true. Which is a decision that will likely haunt Desmond for the rest of his life. But it was a choice between the lemur world and the human world. Ask yourself, if you had been in the same situation, which choice would you have made?

Kitty and her people offered to bridge Desmond, Infinity, and several others to a new world, to live out their lives in peace. Why would they offer this? Now that's a really good question! Why indeed. There must be a very important reason. If you were reading carefully, you know there is another intelligent species living on this new world. Kitty promised that this species was peaceful and would not harm the humans. Was Kitty telling the truth? Is this world the paradise—the neverland—that Infinity and Desmond deserve after all the hell they've been through? All will be revealed in **Bridgers 6**, I promise. **Bridgers 6** should be released in November 2019.

Is Bridgers 6 really going to be the last in the series? Yes, that's my plan at this time. From the beginning, this was planned as a six-book series. After numerous readers requested that Infinity have her own book, I decided to add **INFINITY: A Bridger's Origin** to the series, making a total of seven books. Could I be convinced to write more? Absolutely. But for now, I'm planning a new series, with the first book coming out in early 2020. Don't worry, the new series will involve amazing creatures, mysterious wilderness areas, and plenty of action. And there will even be just the right amount of romance. After all, love is the tie that binds us, right? No matter how different we are. Even if we aren't of the same species (oops, I think I let a hint slip out).

Did Kitty really fix the damage inflicted years ago upon Infinity's reproductive organs? Honestly, I don't know, and neither does Infinity. Again, can Kitty be trusted to tell the truth? Perhaps a more important question is, if Infinity could have a baby, would she want to? After all, she and Desmond are bridging for the last time to live the remainder of their lives on a world they know almost nothing about. This world could turn out to be the last place anyone would ever want to raise a child. But then again, it could be a paradise—a neverland (this is the word bridgers use to describe a safe and picture-perfect world, which, ironically, no bridger has ever found). I did notice that Infinity and Desmond had a rather intimate experience on the picnic table in the park in West Plains, and that was after Kitty performed the procedure. Hmm…

What's the story on this world where Armando has been living for the last nineteen months? At the beginning of **Bridgers 4**, Armando and several other humans managed to escape to a version of Earth that had diverged from their own Earth only 21 years before. What is this new version of Earth like? Since it had diverged from Infinity's version of Earth so recently, the world is very similar. But during the last 21 years, it has been on its own timeline. So you would expect some differences. Different politicians elected to office, for example. One really big event that happened on that world during the last 21 years was a deadly pandemic involving Red Howler Fever (RHF). This pandemic was confined to the United States, but it had a devastating impact on the population and economy. Infinity and Desmond are both older than twenty, so it was possible their other selves could exist on this world. As it turned out, Desmond's other self had been a victim of RHF. Infinity's other self, however, is alive and well. As you know, in **Bridgers 5**, Infinity has the opportunity to talk to her other self, and is surprised to learn that her other self has lived a very different life.

Is it really possible that the earth could implode? This series is based on the destruction of Infinity and Desmond's version of Earth. This is a result of humans using seven bridging devices that have been constructed around the world, including the one at SafeTrek. Unbeknownst to humans, the bridging devices have been emitting a previously-unknown particle.

This particle is heavy and therefore drifts down through the Earth's crust and settles at the Earth's core, the planet's center of gravity. Unfortunately, these particles have a peculiar property: they make every other particle they touch disappear (actually, the substances get bridged to some unknown alternate universe). The result is that, over a period of time, these particles have reduced the mass of the Earth's core. More bridging excursions have resulted in more of these particles, which have resulted in more of the Earth's core disappearing. Eventually, over several years, this began to have an effect on the entire planet. And ultimately, it will result in complete destruction.

The particles created by the bridging devices are obviously fictional (at least I hope they are). And the effects of diminishing the Earth's core can only be based upon speculation. But... people much smarter than me actually *have* speculated about this. If the Earth's core were somehow diminished, one of the first things you could expect to see is unusual and widespread northern lights (aurora borealis). Under normal circumstances, auroras occur near the north and south poles. This is because when the charged particles in the solar wind approach Earth, they are drawn to the magnetic north and south poles, where they interact with atoms and molecules of oxygen, nitrogen and other elements, resulting in a dazzling display of lights in the sky. But the earth's magnetic field is created by the swirling molten metals in the earth's core. If the earth's core is destroyed, so is the earth's magnetic field. So you would start to see auroras all over the earth, not just near the poles. That's why Infinity and Desmond have been seeing auroras even at SafeTrek, which is in Missouri.

You would also expect to experience widespread violent storms (like the super tornadoes in Bridgers 4) and widespread earthquakes. As the Earth's core gets smaller and smaller, these would become more common and more severe. Eventually, due to the pull of gravity, you would experience the mother of all earthquakes (as seen in chapter 1 of **Bridgers 5**) as the earth's crust collapses and falls inward to fill the empty space left behind by the missing core. As you can imagine, no living things would survive this.

Why did Infinity and Desmond's original version of Earth implode while other versions didn't? The humans on Infinity's version of Earth discovered the radio signal from the extraterrestrial civilization known as the Outlanders, which included instructions for constructing bridging devices. The Outlanders at some point in the distant past decided that only certain civilizations should be allowed to exist. Specifically, those civilizations capable of figuring out that the radio signal included a hidden "key" to bridging technology. If a civilization is capable of finding the key, that civilization can then use their bridging devices without destroying their own planet. Without this key, the resulting bridging devices would create the planet-killing particle. Any civilization that discovers the radio signal but not the key would be tempted to construct and use bridging devices, resulting in the death of their civilization. Any civilization that discovers the signal *and* the key is deemed by the Outlanders to be worthy of existing.

There are infinite alternate universes. In some of these universes, the Outlanders don't even exist. In others, the Outlanders exist but never did send out their signal. In others, the Outlanders exist and did send out their signal, but the humans on Earth have not yet discovered the signal. On some versions of Earth, the humans discovered the signal but wisely chose not to construct bridging devices. And on some versions of Earth, humans never even evolved in the first place, and therefore they didn't get the opportunity to discover the signal. With infinite universes, every scenario is possible.

What about other civilizations besides those on various versions of Earth? The Outlanders did not specifically target the Earth. They intended for the signal to go out to other civilizations in their universe, to destroy all civilizations that were becoming highly advanced but did not have a specific ability— the ability to decipher the hidden key. For whatever reason, the Outlanders believed that the ability to decipher this key was a good criterion for being allowed to exist. There is no way to know how many other civilizations, if any, have been destroyed, or will be destroyed in the future, by this cruel plan for "thinning the herd."

The following question has been answered in the Author's Notes in all the other Bridgers books, but I consider it worth including again:

Okay, what about the rather mind-bending concept of the possible existence of infinite parallel universes? While there are certainly cosmologists who are skeptical of the concept, it is important to point out that multiple parallel universes is not a *theory*. Scientists did not simply come up with the idea using their imaginations. Instead, the concept is a mathematical consequence of our current theories in physics, particularly *quantum mechanics* and *string theory*.

If we assume that quantum mechanics and string theory are not completely wrong, then it is important for scientists to examine all of the mathematical consequences of those theories. Even if those consequences (such as parallel universes) seem strange to us. This is often how science moves forward.

There are at least five plausible scientific theories that suggest the existence of multiple universes (the "multiverse"). My favorite of these is the concept of "daughter universes" suggested by the theory of quantum mechanics. Quantum mechanics describes things in terms of probabilities, rather than definite outcomes. The mathematics of quantum mechanics suggest that every possible outcome of every situation actually occurs—in its own separate universe.

Everything is made up of tiny particles, and what this "daughter universes" concept boils down to is that there could be infinite parallel universes, each of them differing by the position of only one particle.

The concept boggles the mind. But it certainly makes for a fun story.

ACKNOWLEDGMENTS

I am not capable of creating a book such as this on my own. I have the following people, among others, to thank for their assistance.

When it comes to editing, my son Micheal Smith is extremely talented, and his tireless and meticulous suggestions are invaluable. If you find a sentence or detail in the book that doesn't seem right, it is likely because I failed to implement one of his suggestions.

My wife Trish is always the first to read my work, and therefore she has the burden of seeing my stories in their roughest form. Thankfully, she kindly points out where things are a mess. Her suggestions are what get the editing process started. She also helps with various promotional efforts. And finally, she not only tolerates my obsession with writing, she actually encourages it.

I also owe thanks to those on my Advance Reviewer team. They were able to point out numerous typos and inconsistencies.

Finally, I am thankful to all the independent freelance designers out there who provide quality work for independent authors such as myself. Jake Caleb Clark (www.jcalebdesign.com) created the awesome cover for *Bridgers 5: The Trial of Extinction*.

ABOUT THE AUTHOR

Stan Smith has lived most of his life in the Midwest United States and currently resides with his wife Trish in a home nestled within an Ozark forest near Warsaw, Missouri. He writes adventure novels and short stories that have a generous sprinkling of science fiction. His novels and stories are about regular people who find themselves caught up in highly unusual situations. They are designed to stimulate your sense of wonder, get your heart pounding, and keep you reading late into the night, with minimal risk of exposure to spelling and punctuation errors. His books are for anyone who loves adventure, discovery, and mind-bending surprises.

Stan's Author Website
http://www.stancsmith.com

Feel free to email Stan at: stan@stancsmith.com
He loves hearing from readers and will answer every email.

ALSO BY STAN C. SMITH

The DIFFUSION series

Diffusion

Infusion

Profusion

Savage

Blue Arrow

Diffusion Box Set

The BRIDGERS series

Bridgers 1: The Lure of Infinity

Bridgers 2: The Cost of Survival

Bridgers 3: The Voice of Reason

Bridgers 4: The Mind of Many

Bridgers 5: The Trial of Extinction

Bridgers 6: The Bond of Absolution

INFINITY: A Bridger's Origin

Bridgers 1-3 Box Set

Bridgers 4-6 Box Set

The ACROSS HORIZONS series

1: Obsolete Theorem

2. Foregone Conflict

3. Hostile Emergence

4. Binary Existence
Prequel: Genesis Sequence

The FUSED series
Prequel: Training Day
1. Rampage Ridge
2. Primordial Pit

Stand-alone Stories
Parthenium's Year